THE ROCKPORT RUBIES

Rupert, the new Duke of Jordans, appears blessed
with good fortune. Possessed of many acres of
Mallamshire and a stately home filled with the loot of
three centuries, with a pretty wife and two fine sons,
why should he be driven to disrupt what looks like a
golden future?

His problems start with his stepmother Sheila,
Duchess of Jordans, who refuses to yield the family
heirlooms – including the fabled Rockport Rubies –
since she sees in them a means of securing herself a
lush future. She is residing at the house of an
American friend, Betty Bassano, and, during the
prolonged negotiations with his stepmother, Rupert
finds himself embarking on an affair with the
handsome, wealthy Betty.

Meanwhile, at Rockport Place, Rupert's wife feels
isolated in a strange, vast house, surrounded by an
entrenched and forbidding staff; she turns to an old
family friend, the redoubtable Dame Elizabeth de
Blete, but even she, with all her diplomatic skills,
finds it hard to effect a reconciliation whilst saving
the face of all concerned.

The Rockport Rubies

A Mallamshire novel

ROSAMOND FITZROY

ROBERT HALE · LONDON

© Rosamond Fitzroy 1989
First published in Great Britain 1989

ISBN 0 7090 3639 6

Robert Hale Limited
Clerkenwell House
Clerkenwell Green
London EC1R 0HT

Photoset in North Wales by
Derek Doyle & Associates, Mold, Clwyd.
Printed in Great Britain by
St Edmundsbury Press Ltd, Bury St Edmunds, Suffolk.
Bound by WBC Bookbinders Limited.

Extract from Debrett

JORDANS, DUKE OF

JAMES GEORGE HENRY DELANEY-GREY, 10th Duke, b.1922, s.1979; ed. at Eton. Served war 1939-45 The Mallamshires (Capt); m. 1st, 1944 (m. diss. 1980) Lorna May, dau. of Robert T. Decker of Los Angeles; 2ndly 1980 Sheila Lady Fiske (see Fiske, Bt.) and has issue by 1st m.
Seat: Rockport Place, Mallamshire. *Address*: c/o PO Box 338912 Nassau, Bahamas.

Sons living
RUPERT (*Earl of Rockport*) b. 1945. Ed. at Stowe. m. 1978 Diana, only da. of Squadron Leader and Mrs W. Squires and has issue – Charles William George (*Lord Somersham*) b. 1982, Hon. Jonathan James b. 1984. *Residence* Byegrove, Sweet Madrigal, Mallamshire.
Lord Colin, b. 1950, *ed.* at Stowe. *Address:* c/o The Dower House, Rockport.

Widow living of son of 10th Duke
Hon. Sybil (*Countess of Kilmourne*) da. of 19th Baron Ingrams; m. 1969 Charles Henry (*Earl of Kilmourne*) who d. 1980 and has issue – *Lady* Jane Lorna, b. 1973, *Lady* Mary Alice, b. 1976. *Residence* Jordanstown, Ireland.

Sisters living

Lady Alice, b. 1924, m. 1945 Mark Brinscomb, 4th Baron Brinscomb (see that title). Address: Bishop's Malford Manor, Mallamshire.

Lady Margaret, b. 1927, m. 1947 Matthew Wright (Wrighton Manor, Mallamshire) and has issue Mark Delaney, b. 1950, m. 1986 Jean, da. of Dr and Mrs A.P. Mackintosh. *Residence* Home Farm, Wrighton, Mallamshire.

Predecessors

(1) Sir Charles Grey, KG, natural son of Charles II by Effie Grey, b. 1664, cr *Baron Grey, Earl of Kilmourne* and *Duke of Jordans* (peerage of Ireland) 1680. m. 1680 Mary O'Giordain of Jordanstown, Ireland: d. 1710; s. by his son (2) JAMES, 2nd Duke, d. 1740; s. by his son (3) CHARLES, 3rd Duke, b. 1720, m. Elizabeth Bowen, d. 1760; s. by his son (4) JAMES, 4th Duke, b. 1751, m. 1771 Serena, da. and heiress of James Delaney of Rockport House, Mallamshire: cr. 1780 *Earl of Rockport* and *Baron Somersham* (peerage of England), d. 1831, s. by his son (5) CHARLES, 5th Duke, b. 1774, d. 1837, s. by his brother (6) ROBERT, 6th Duke, b. 1780, d. 1848, s. by his son (7) CHARIES, KG, PC, 7th Duke, attached to Earl Granville's Embassy to Russia 1856, a Lord of the Admiralty 1858, Secretary of State for War 1868-70, m. 1845 Amelia, da. of Lord Henry Cecil, d. 1888, s. by his son (8) JAMES, b. 1846, 8th Duke, m. 1885 Anne, da. of Henry Franks, Lord Lt. Mallamshire, High Steward Greyabbey, d. 1922, s. by his son (9) CHARLES HENRY GEORGE, GCVO, GBE, m. 1920 Lady Sophia Kidderminster, Lord Lt. Mallamshire, High Steward, Greyabbey, Hon. Col. Mallamshire Yeomanry, d. 1979, s. by his son (10) JAMES GEORGE HENRY, 10th Duke and present peer: also Earl of Rockport, Earl of Kilmourne, Baron Somersham and Baron Grey.

One

It is still, even in this age of equality, a fine thing to be an English Duke. In his prime, blessed with many opulent acres of Mallamshire, a splendid mansion house filled with the loot of past centuries, a pretty wife and two fine boys, this was the station to which Rupert, eleventh Duke of Jordans, ascended after the death of his father.

The Most Noble Rupert James Robert Delaney-Grey, Duke of Jordans, Earl of Rockport, Earl of Kilmourne, Baron Somersham and Baron Grey, was then in his forty-third year. Slight of build, and with wide-eyed features like those of a monkey, he had a ready, open smile and his manner was unassuming, the sonorous roll of his titles signifying to him only an expression of his family's history. His modesty may have been due to the fact that, as a second son, he had not been in line for the inheritance; it had been necessary for him to make his own living, and only after the sudden death of his elder brother, known by courtesy as the Earl of Kilmourne, who had no sons, did Rupert return to Mallamshire as heir apparent, assuming for himself the title that his father had used before him, Lord Rockport. Nor had his wife Diana been born to the strawberry leaves: her father, a retired squadron leader, was the licensee of the Rockport Arms, a well-known and expensive hostelry. Rupert's mother had been opposed to the match; but the young were deeply in love, and determined; more, they had the quiet support of many friends in the county, and when Rupert's great-aunt Euphemia took their side and provided them with a home at Byegrove, a Jacobean manor seven miles from Rockport, the wedding took place in the chapel of his grandfather's house, the massively Palladian Rockport Place.

Hostilities had not lasted long. Lorna Jordans, Rupert's mother, was American by birth and outlook: she soon came to see that her antagonism to Diana's background was nothing more than snobbery, and inconsistent with her republican upbringing: as she began to recognise the steady love the girl felt for her son, and to acknowledge Diana's common sense and readiness to work, there grew between them a firm affection. Lorna's approval became admiration when, after her divorce from Rupert's father and his departure to the Bahamas, Rupert and Diana began to undertake, willingly and well, the many duties that fell their way out and about the county. Invitations to open fêtes, to chair committees for worthy causes, to lend their name to this and to that, flooded in, their influence was beginning to be felt where it mattered and already word was about that Rupert's name might soon be pricked to serve his term as High Sheriff of Mallamshire.

The divorce was now, after nine years, a thing of the past as far as the county was concerned; but Rupert had not forgotten the bitterness and disruption it had caused. Because of it, he and Diana had been forced into public life and to forswear the years of tranquillity that they might have enjoyed while they established their family and made firm their marriage. He still felt a dislike for the woman who had caused it all.

Her name had been Sheila, Lady Fiske. The impoverished widow of a baronet, she had happened to encounter Jamey Jordans on the down train from London; but they had known each other before, years ago at the end of the war, when Jamey had been a dapper young subaltern about London and Sheila a pretty Wren. The affair had prospered. At first, Lorna had been tolerant: Jamey had enjoyed flings before, and she was preoccupied with preparing Rockport Place to be opened to the public. So when Jamey finally faced up to her and told her he wanted a divorce so that he might marry Sheila, Lorna had been, first, aghast, and then very resolute. If he wanted to go off with Sheila, she couldn't stop him; but she was damned if she would just step aside and permit that fluffy little woman to step into her shoes at Rockport. She had put much effort – and a great many dollars – into the restoration of the great house, and her father had sent over from California his famous Museum of Motion Picture Memorabilia which, housed in the former orangery, formed a major attraction for the paying visitors. She wasn't going to hand all that over to Sheila without a fight.

In the end, the Jordans trustees had come down in Lorna's favour. The trustees, akin to a board of directors, controlled the elaborate network of discretionary settlements and holding companies that sustained the wealth of the dukedom: the lands, both in Mallamshire and in Ireland, a few hundred square yards of London that had once been a market garden, even the major pictures and objets d'art and the heirloom jewellery, all were wrapped up by the trustees, safe from the depradations of the tax authorities and from the wanton extravagance of a spendthrift Duke.

Jamey and Sheila hadn't a chance. The trustees, looking to the future, handed over the running of the Rockport estate to Rupert, and confirmed Lorna in her occupancy of the Dower House for her lifetime. As for Jamey, provided he went into tax exile, they declared that he would continue to enjoy a substantial income: and they undertook to make suitable provision for his wife.

On a misty morning in October, standing in the great

saloon at Rockport Place and surrounded by the portraits of his predecessors, Rupert did not feel himself changed since he now was, and had been for a week, duke. Standing at one of the tall sash windows that overlooked the sweep of parkland dotted with trees, their branches still and stark black in the grey haze, that rolled down to a serpentine lake with, on the far side and just visible in the murk, a small white domed temple, he realised that he felt somehow that he was come home.

He grinned at the thought. The vast mansion, with its pillared portico, its vaulted galleries and richly plastered state rooms, was few people's idea of a home these days. But it was all familiar to him: he had been much concerned with the restoration work. Before his marriage, he had earned his living as an art dealer, and his expertise had come in very useful when it came to rehanging the many treasures that formed his heritage. It was already more his place than it had ever been his father's: in fact, the tenth duke had not spent a night at Rockport since the war.

Rupert felt no deep grief for his father: little more than a sadness. Once they had been on good terms; but distance, time and Sheila intervening had made them drift apart. Still, he remembered, it had been a shock when, seven days ago, Sheila had telephoned from Nassa with the news that Jamey had succumbed to a sudden heart attack. He had at once offered to fly to the Bahamas, but his stepmother told him it was quite unnecessary: she was perfectly capable of arranging a funeral and cremation. Then, Rupert had suggested, he must at least lay on a memorial service in Mallamshire; to this, Sheila consented, and the organisation of such a service was the reason for Rupert's presence at Rockport Place this Monday morning. Monday was the only day when the house was never open to visitors, which was why he had the great saloon to himself, as he waited for his mother, his wife and his brother to join him in a family conference.

'Good morning, Your Grace,' a rich sepulchral voice intoned at exactly the right pitch to travel the length of the hall. Rupert turned round to see, at the far end and across the wide expanse of black and white marble, a black-clad figure standing at the tall double mahogany doors. This was Dobson, the family butler, and Rupert returned the greeting with affection, noting that it was the first time the old man had addressed him in style.

'Her Grace has telephoned from the Dower House, Your Grace,' Dobson announced, relishing the formalities, 'and she requested me to inform you that Lord Colin has only just arrived from London. Her Grace and His Lordship will be here in twenty minutes.'

'Thank you, Dobson. Perhaps we might have some coffee in the business-room. My wife – that is to say Her Grace – will be here in a few minutes.'

'Very good, Your Grace.' The butler gave a slight inclination of the head. 'I have already instructed James to light the fire.'

Rupert smiled. He was very fond of the old man, who had been a fixture at Rockport for as long as he could remember. As butler to his grandfather, Dobson had been a friend to the young and callow Rupert Delaney-Grey, conniving at his pranks and high spirits: on one such occasion, he had held an impromptu party for a gang of his friends in the cavernous kitchen downstairs. He had been discovered by the butler in the middle of the night but Dobson had winked at the intrusion; and it was, Rupert recalled, the first time he had taken out the pretty girl who was now his wife.

Dobson was showing his age. Although the portly frame still filled the formal black jacket, the sleek head of hair and the bushy eyebrows were quite white, and he stood in the doorway with a pronounced stoop. But then, Rupert reflected, James, who had been footman, was now crippled with arthritis, and Aggie Smiles, the one-time cook, was almost immobile, spending her days squatting like a fat toad beside her ever-burning Aga.

With the great house open to the public, the position of the old domestic staff was equivocal. The duke was in exile, his former wife lived in the Dower House and his son and heir over at Bygrove: Rockport Place was no longer where the family lived, merely a museum that came to life only during visiting hours. It would have been most practical to have retired the servants, to have found them cottages or rooms in the village and pensioned them off; but Rupert had insisted, that would have been cruel. All their working lives, they had lived and served in the house: they were close-knit, like a family. Each had a private domain: Aggie her kitchen, Dobson his pantry and James the former boot-room, which they domesticated and made cosy, with their personal possessions about them: and in the servants' hall, which had once seated twenty senior staff, they convened in the evenings to watch television and to murmur together about the old days.

So they stayed on. At first, Dobson, and James were recruited to assist as guardians, watching over the state rooms as the viewing public trooped past. Dobson had rather enjoyed this: taking up his stance by the vast William Kent sideboard in the blue dining-room, he stood immobile yet watchful, as if he were still presiding over the service of some grand state dinner of the past. The trouble was that neither he nor James was sufficiently well informed to answer the many questions asked by the paying public, and they would not condescend to chatter with those they regarded as invaders and beneath their notice. After an incident involving some chewing gum applied to a silver-framed photograph of Queen Alexandra, which resulted in a cuff about the ears for the snivelling culprit and a forceful complaint from its parents, the Comptroller,

Mr De Blete, put his foot down. Mr de Blete was responsible for the enterprise that ran the stately home side of the household and in future guiding, he said, must be left to the troupe of trained and often garrulous ladies whom he had recruited from the nearby town of Somersham.

Rupert knew that the old staff were hoping that his accession might lead to changes in the house, that perhaps things might revert to the old days, when the place was filled with the family and their friends and not with gaping intruders. Hence the old butler's rare appearance as a household functionary: hence the even more unusual provision of a fire in the business-room. Well, change there would be: he and Diana had already decided; but it was for Diana to take charge of her household and to inform them of her dispositions when the time was right. So, with another kindly word, he dismissed Dobson and ambled over to the chimneypiece that dominated the north wall of the saloon.

It was of white marble, vast, and carved into the entablature was a relief of Apollo riding the sun. Above, in an ornately gilded frame, was a portrait by Sir Peter Lely with the inscription 'The Maid of Old Holborn'. It showed an ample young woman, draped in red velvet that made the most of her rosy, voluptuous curves; her face was not beautiful, nor even pretty, but it was alight with the joy of living and with, Rupert felt, a deliciously wry humour. He knew the painting well, for it was of his ancestress, who had been Effie Grey.

Effie had been an actress at the time of the Restoration, known to her public as the Maid of Old Holborn (until recently, there was a pub of that name not far from the viaduct). Catching the libidinous eye of her monarch, in due time she bore him a son, named after his royal father; but by 1670, Effie had died of the plague, and young Charley Grey grew up by his wits on the shadowy fringes of the court. When the bastard was

sixteen, and a handsome lad, he drew the attention of
his father: Charles II was always generous to his
progeny: a marriage was arranged to an Irish heiress
and Charley Grey suddenly found himself Duke of
Jordans and Earl of Kilmourne in the peerage of
Ireland, settling on his wife's lands at Jordanstown, not
far from Lough Neagh. During the subsequent reigns,
and especially after the Hanoverians came to the
throne, the Dukes of Jordans remained at Jordanstown,
growing steadily poorer.

In 1770 the fourth Duke went to London, hoping to
redeem his dwindling fortune. He had one connection,
his kinsman the Duke of Grafton, who by luck was
Prime Minister at the time; and through him he was
found a well-endowed wife with a dowry to match his
august rank. Serena Delaney brought with her name
some useful acres of West London and vast estates in
Mallamshire; and to signify the suitability of the match
(and to enable the Duke to play his part in political life)
the Earldom of Rockport and the Barony of Somersham were added to the Irish honorifics.

By all accounts, the marriage had been a success.
Certainly, the portrait by Gainsborough which Rupert
was now studying suggested a couple happy in each
other's company. The young Duchess, in a pink,
sprigged dress, is seated by an arbour, with the Duke
attentively bending over her and their children spread
decorously at their feet. In the background stood the
creamy white facade of Rockport Place, with its
Corinthian columns, its row of statues crowning the
balustrade and its wings running out to embrace twin
pavilions, all new-built by the fourth Duke on the site of
an Elizabethan manor to mark his accession to fortune
and to Mallamshire.

The other portraits in the saloon marked the dynastic
descent of the Delaney-Greys: a fine Lawrence of
Charles, fifth Duke and the little boy in a blue dress in

the Gainsborough, a pretty Winterhalter of Amelia, wife of the seventh Duke, and a pleasing brown study of the ninth Duke by Sir William Orpen were Rupert's favourites, especially the last, for he would never forget that it had been the intervention of his grandfather that had made possible his marriage to Diana here in the chapel of Rockport Place.

A scrunch on the gravelled forecourt outside now drew Rupert's attention. Diana had arrived in her estate car: dressed in her countrywoman's outfit of green quilted jacket, headscarf, tweed skirt and sensible brown brogues. She dismounted. Rupert waved through the window and then went round to the side door to let her in.

As Diana untied her headscarf and shook out her hair, Rupert took her coat and hung it on a hatstand, made from the stuffed head of an elk, that lurked in a dark corner of the lobby.

'I thought I'd never get here,' she was saying. 'Charley went off willingly enough, but Jonathan made a fearful fuss. He usually enjoys play-school: I suppose it was just a tantrum.'

Charley was their elder son, now aged seven and attending the village school at Sweet Madrigal, near Byegrove. Since he was born, he had been gazetted as Lord Somersham, while his younger brother, who was four, was named Jonathan. Both parents were agreed that the boys should enjoy as normal an upbringing as possible: their titles were never used and their playmates were their friends from the village.

Rupert grinned at his wife as she turned to kiss him. She was short, with a trim figure and an erect carriage: her dark hair fell softly from a peak that divided her wide, clear brow, giving her triangular face the shape of a heart; but for all her prettiness, there was steadiness and determination in her large dark blue eyes, and the line of her jaw was firm. She took her husband's arm

and they walked together back through the great
saloon, through double doors and into the chamber
known as the green drawing-room, where Rupert
paused.

'We're taking on an awful lot,' he murmured. 'I
suppose we have made the right decision?'

'Of course we have,' Diana assured him, squeezing his
arm. 'I must admit I'm a bit daunted, but we have
agreed it's the right thing to do.'

In this room were hung the most precious items in the
Jordans heritage: a rich and sensuous Caravaggio of
Venus attended by some muscular, half-draped
demi-gods, and, in complete contrast, a tranquil
Madonna by Giovanni Bellini.

'At least it will be good to live in the same house as
these two,' said Rupert. 'We'll be able to pay them a call
every day.'

'Provided it's not during opening hours,' Diana teased
him, pointing to the braided rope which kept the paying
public to their appointed path. They followed the rope
along the enfilade of state rooms that filled the north
front of the house, through the crimson boudoir and
the Queen's bedroom, prepared for a visit by Queen
Adelaide and never since slept in, and so to the
business-room, where the family conference awaited
them.

Two

'Who on earth,' drawled Lorna Duchess of Jordans, 'is Mrs Betty Bassano?'

They were gathered in the business-room, Rupert at his desk, his mother in a chair beside it, his wife perched on the sofa and his brother Lord Colin straddling the club fender. Dobson had supervised while James made a ritual of serving the coffee; once the old servants had withdrawn, Rupert began to explain the plans that were being made for the memorial service: he had just divulged that his stepmother Sheila had told him, on the telephone that morning, that she had every intention of attending the service, and that she would be staying in Mallamshire with her old friend Betty Bassano.

'Sheila spoke as if I ought to know her,' Rupert answered, 'but I've never heard of a Mrs Bassano.'

All four faces were blank, and Diana suggested that perhaps Jean might know.

'Good idea,' said Rupert, reaching for the intercom. Jean Wright was his secretary; a doctor's daughter from Luckton Malford, she had married Rupert's cousin Mark Wright who farmed over beyond Roman Cross, and was a fount of knowledge about property in the county.

'Jean?' Rupert spoke into the machine. 'I've just heard from my stepmother that she proposes to stay for the service with a Mrs Betty Bassano. Have you heard anything about her?'

'I think so,' Jean's clear voice came back. 'I think that's the name of the American who bought Lordstanding in the spring. Word is that she is loaded, without a husband, and has spent a king's ransom on doing up the house.'

'That must be the one,' said Rupert, 'thank you, Jean,' and he clicked off the machine.

'Lordstanding,' he murmured, 'I remember it was advertised in *Country Life*. It was put on the market after old Mrs Mannering died. It looked like a lovely place, I must say: it's on the river, up beyond Shipston.'

'Have you heard of her, Lorna?' Diana asked. Lorna, being herself American by birth, might be expected to have some knowledge of the unknown; but Lorna shook her head.

'The trouble with us Americans is that one never knows who they marry,' she said, a hint of a transatlantic twang in her voice. Lorna Duchess of Jordans was tall and elegant in a soft grey jersey dress; her hair was almost white now, but very stylish, and with her arched eyebrows and long, delicate nose she had an air of distinction.

'If I knew who her father was, or one of her husbands, then I'd have a clue about her money – old or new, Jewish or Ivy League. In the States, money is what genealogy is to the British.'

'Well, whoever she is, I'm grateful to Mrs Bassano,' Diana put in. 'At least, we don't have to have Sheila to stay at Byegrove: that might have been awkward. As it is, we must have her over for lunch or dinner: she is Jamey's widow, when all is said and done.'

'Quite right, my dear,' said Lorna, looking at her daughter-in-law with approval, 'and while Sheila is here, I'll lie low.'

'Do you mean, Mother, that you won't come to the service?' Colin looked surprised.

'Oh, no. That must be Sheila's day. I'll take myself to

London. I just hope she doesn't stay too long in Mallamshire.'

Now they were back on the subject of the service, Rupert told them that Canon Pew-Brown, an old family friend, had agreed to officiate, assisted by the Vicar of Rockport. The estate workers and tenants would attend, family friends informed, and both the High Sheriff and the Lord Lieutenant had signified their intention to be present. For all that his father had not been much in Mallamshire, Rupert was resolved that the tenth Duke's last farewell to the county should be well attended.

'... and I think, Colin, that it might be a courtesy if you collected Sheila from Lordstanding and escorted her to the church.'

Lord Colin nodded agreement. He was a thin man, in his thirties, taller than his brother, and with sparse fair hair. He had inherited the finely chiselled features of his mother, translated into a bony masculinity. Lorna sometimes worried that, despite a succession of girlfriends brought down to the Dower House for weekends, Colin had not yet married: he seemed to live a prosperous but self-contained life in London, where he worked on the Baltic Exchange.

'Darling, you said the church.' Diana looked puzzled. 'Aren't we going to use the chapel?'

She had happy memories of the chapel, an early Victorian creation inserted into one of the pavilions of the house: it was there that, thanks to Rupert's grandfather, her wedding had taken place.

'Not on this occasion,' her husband answered. 'We've always used the village church for funerals, and a lot of us are buried in the graveyard there. In any case, the chapel is too small.'

As he made these dispositions, with his family around him and attentive to his words, it came to him for the first time that he was indeed the head, and regarded as such even by his mother. Sitting at his grandfather's desk, he was aware too of a strong sense of continuity. In his mind, he still carried a vision of the portraits at which he had earlier been looking, and they seemed to reinforce his feeling that not only his nearest and dearest but all his predecessors were watching as he assumed the reins.

It gave him confidence that they were in the business-room. In his grandfather's day it had been known as the small library, and very much the old man's sanctum, where, when indoors, he spent most of his time, warmed only by the inadequate bars of an ancient electric fire. Beyond were the echoing, chilly chambers, halls and corridors of the vast palace, only called into use on rare great occasions: in here, the ninth Duke had attended to estate business and his correspondence.

When Lorna Jordans took over, she had assumed the room for herself, keeping only the desk: she had installed the intercom and the telephones, arranged the serried ranks of efficiently labelled box-files on the shelves which had once held bound volumes of *The Parliamentary Companion*, *The Illustrated London News* and the *Badminton Library*. In due course, as Rupert assumed more responsibility, Lorna had handed over the room to her son: he in turn had started to fill it with his own interests, books of art criticism and history and a row of huge leather ledgers, past inventories of the possessions of his family into which he was presently researching.

As she had changed the room, bringing it into the twentieth century, so Lorna had transformed the house. Her energies – and an ample flow of her own dollars – had been devoted first to the structure of the house, which, with dry-rot eliminated, a programme of re-roofing completed and the installation of ample heating and an efficient security system, was now as sound as it had ever been. She had then proceeded to convert the old sculleries into a teashop for the visitors, named 'Effie Grey's Pantry', provided public lavatories, spreading car parks, and a gift shop. Lorna's contribution had been generous, which was why, when she divorced, the trustees had refused to consider permitting her ex-husband to take up residence; and it was also why Rupert was hesitating before he told her what he and Diana had in mind.

'Diana and I have something to say,' he began, 'and we very much hope, Mother, that our plan will have your blessing. Put simply, it is that we intend to move back into Rockport Place and to make this house our home.'

'It hasn't been an easy decision,' Diana added. 'We both love Byegrove, and have been very happy there. But we feel we ought to be here: the house needs to be a family home, and not a dead museum.'

'With all respect to what you have done, Mother,' Rupert went on, 'we are convinced that now I have succeeded, our place is at Rockport.'

'My dears,' said Lorna, 'I can't think why you're worried about my feelings. I've done my bit for Rockport and been glad to, but I'm most relieved that Rupert has now taken over the responsibility of running the place. I must say I think it's a brave decision that you've taken, for it won't be easy, but I do know it is the right decision. Rockport Place is meant to be home to the Duke and his family: when it is that again, it will once more be a living house.'

Thus given his mother's blessing, Rupert led them happily into a discussion of what needed to be done, where the nurseries should best be placed, how to instal a new kitchen.

'For everyday use, I thought we would use the octagonal room on the east front for dining,' said Diana. 'Then the new kitchen could be fitted in behind that, with access to the courtyard: and when we have a big occasion and need to use the state dining-room, it will be a simple matter to close it to the public.'

'We also want to use the library on the south side as our own living-room,' Rupert put in, 'so that must be taken off the visitors' route; and Diana will use the Dutch parlour next to it as her own sitting-room.'

'You've worked it all out, I see,' said Lorna with a smile, 'but I must warn you, there may well be problems with the staff. We've just seen Dobson and James doing their best to go back to what they think of as the good old days. And I'm not sure they could cope with a young family here.'

'They won't have to.' Diana was decisive: she had trained in the hotel business and considered herself used to dealing with domestics. 'I'm going to have my own people to look after us: Molly Platt loves the boys as much as we do, and she has run Byegrove for me very smoothly. She'll be our housekeeper; and I've told her that she can always draw on Dobson and James when we have a big dinner party.'

'We think it best to leave the servants' hall as it is: the old dears don't want to be disturbed. They can potter about as they've done since Grandfather died.' Rupert was happy to leave this side of their new regime to his wife: and he wanted to move on to his next piece of news.

On the fender, the thin face of Colin Delaney-Grey had grown increasingly bored as his brother went on about the new domestic arrangements. He now stood up and stretched himself.

'Well, Rupert,' he said, 'I wish you and Diana good luck; but it's of no concern to me, so I think I might as well push back to London. I'll be down again the night before the service.'

'Just a minute, Colin. Rockport Place is your concern: at least, I hope it will be when you've heard me out.'

Rupert looked round the room, as if to gather their attention to him.

'As you all know, strictly speaking, I don't own any of

this: in the eyes of the law, it all belongs to the various trusts which over the years have been established to hold the real estate and the chattels associated with our family. My grandmother used to serve as the family representative on the board: since her death, the position has been vacant, and we hope, Colin, that you will accept an invitation to become a trustee.'

'Why me? I'm a busy man: I have my living to earn, and none of the trusts are any of my business.' Colin was well aware that, as a younger son, he wouldn't enjoy much in the tidal flow of benefits: as was customary in such families, primogeniture was all.

'Well, for one thing, there isn't anyone else. Mother has already declined the job.'

'That's right,' Lorna drawled. 'For one thing I want to draw in my horns, and for another, it wouldn't be altogether suitable. I'm only the former wife of the Duke, and it might be embarrassing if I was a trustee and had to decide on some matter concerning Sheila. Anyway, I think Colin will fill the post very well.'

'I'll do it then,' Colin assented; and Rupert ticked off an item on the paper in front of him.

'I'm glad you've accepted, because I have to seek the trustees' consent to moving in: and I have to negotiate a fair rent. And' – he tapped the next item on his list – 'I want to arrange a display of the Rockport rubies in the crimson boudoir, and they'll have to agree to that as well.'

'The Rockport rubies?' Lorna arched her eyebrows. 'I haven't seen them for years. I presume they are in the vaults in London with the rest of the heirloom jewellery. I remember your grandmother wore them to the coronation.'

'And we had them out a year or so ago,' Diana said. 'Don't you remember, darling? I displayed them at the Red Cross ball, and then I had them on again when we went to a party at Harvestone.'

'Yes, and I took them back to town for you,' Colin put in.

'Well, I need them out again,' said Rupert. 'I have to show them to an expert.'

'Whatever for?' Diana asked the question that was in all their minds. She remembered the rubies well: in the form of a parure, they made up into a heavy necklace and matching ear-rings set with diamonds. Splendid they might be, but they had also been very uncomfortable to wear, and she had been glad to return them to safe storage. There was, she recalled, a large stone in the form of a ruby the size of a quail's egg that made a droplet in the middle of the ornate necklace, and some kind of family legend went with it.

'Is it because of the stone that Charles II gave Effie Grey?' she added.

'Oh no,' Rupert was dismissive, 'that's just romantic eyewash. I think I may have proved their real provenance and it's much more exciting. Did you ever take a look at a painting of Aphrodite that used to hang on the landing above the oak staircase?'

Lorna, whose knowledge of the big house and its contents was good, answered. 'Very dirty, and badly lit? Yes, I know the one. It was labelled "Caravaggio", but obviously wasn't, so we just assumed it was a nineteenth-century copy.'

'That's the one,' said Rupert with enthusiasm, 'and all the inventories for the last hundred years have ignored it as insignificant. But I've been back further, and I've found a ledger that lists all the items sent back from Rome after the death of the fifth Duke, who married an Italian and made his home there. Among them is a painting entitled *Venus and the Tribute of Love*: and the ledger names Hannibal Carracci as the painter.'

Diana had no idea of the drift of Rupert's story, but she did pick up one clue.

'Isn't the tribute in the picture a casket of jewels?' she

asked. 'They spill out all round Venus's feet, among some gambolling cherubs.'

'Yes, but you're ahead of the story,' said Rupert impatiently. 'First I must tell you about Annibale Carracci, who lived at the end of the sixteenth century. One of his patrons was a Cardinal Marezzo, whose so-called niece – probably his daughter – married into the Malavicini. There are contemporary accounts of the young Countess Malavicini flaunting a fabulous necklace of red stones all round Rome, and suggestions that it was a wedding present from the then Pope, Paul V, who was a Borghese.'

Rupert was enjoying the display of his learning; but his brother was impatient.

'Okay,' Colin said, 'the Malavicini jewels might have something to do with the Rockport rubies: but can you prove it?'

'I think so. We know that the necklace was famous in Rome: what could have been more natural than for Carracci to have flattered his patron by using, in his painting, the actual rubies. That's why I want to show them to the Dutch expert: if he confirms that the setting is Renaissance, then we're half-way home: a visual comparison should do the rest.'

'It's a fine tale,' said Lorna, 'but you haven't told us how the stones came into our family.'

'That's simple.' Rupert was ready for this. 'By the end of the eighteenth century, the Malavicini had more or less died out. There was just one daughter; and in 1801, during a lull in the Napoleonic Wars, she married Charles, then Earl of Rockport and subsequently the 5th Duke of Jordans.

'The fifth Duke has always been something of a mystery: there's no portrait of him, nor of his wife, and he's hardly mentioned in the archives. He turned Catholic and lived out his life in Rome, making over the English estates to his brother. He had no children and after he died, there's a good deal of acrimonious correspondence in the muniments-room between the sixth Duke and the British envoy in Rome about shipping home all the contents of the Palazzo Malavicini. I'm convinced that that's how the rubies and the painting came into our family.'

'Thanks for the history lesson,' said Colin, 'but I still don't see why you're so het up.'

'You can take it from me,' said Rupert, 'that the discovery of a new and important Carracci will be big news in the art world. The story of its provenance should give us world coverage. And if we put it on display alongside the very jewels that Carracci painted, Rockport Place will really hit the headlines.'

'My dear, that's most exciting,' said Lorna, 'I do congratulate you.' To herself, she was thinking how different was her son's attitude from her own: when she had embarked on the opening of the great house, her own big attraction had been the display of her father's remarkable collection of cinematic treasures. There was a world of difference between such items as the original sledge from *Citizen Kane*, a section of the actual Yellow Brick Road and one of Miss Shirley Temple's dancing-pumps, and the Renaissance treasures that Rupert had discovered. She hoped that the latter weren't going to prove a little too eclectic for the taste of the great British public; but it was none of her business now: Rupert was in charge and she was content to take a back seat. Instead, she proposed that they all adjourned to the Dower House for luncheon.

When they came out into the gravelled forecourt, the autumn mist had dispersed and the air was still warm. Pale sunlight washed the facade of the great house gold and laid long shadows across the green grass of the deer park. The drive curled away in a wide curve to cross the glinting waters of the lake by way of an elegant stone bridge before climbing the slope beyond. At the top stood the Dower House, Lorna's home, prettily decked out in the Gothick taste of the Regency. They strolled down the drive in pairs, Diana by Colin's side and Rupert with his mother.

'Have you decided what you're going to do with Byegrove?' Colin asked his sister-in-law, to whom he was very attached.

'Not yet. It belongs to us, you know, and isn't part of any trust, but we'd like to keep it in the family. I don't suppose you'd like to live there, would you, Colin? It's time you thought about settling down.'

She looked up at his thin face, driven by the urge in all contented wives to marry off those of whom they are fond.

'No fear, not yet.' He grinned at her. 'I have my living to earn in London, not like you idle plutocrats down here.'

'We're not idle!' She rose to his teasing. 'You should see my diary; and the move is going to take a lot of organisation. And,' she confessed, 'I haven't told Rupert, but some aspects of living here terrify me.'

'Such as?' he asked, taking her arm for comfort.

'Dobson, for example. He has only to beetle his beastly eyebrows at me and I'm reduced to a quivering jelly, like some sluttish scullery maid who's dropped a silver candlestick. I'm terrified at the thought of having to give him orders.'

'Old Dobson is all right,' said Colin, who, like his brother, had happy memories of the butler's indulgence to him as a boy. 'Anyway, he's more or less retired now: if you organise things, you shouldn't have much to do with him.'

'I hope so,' said Diana doubtfully.

The other two, meanwhile, had reached the bridge and here they paused, looking back at the spreading arms of the palace on its hill.

'I hope you will both be very happy here,' Lorna said

quietly, 'and the boys too. By the way, you haven't yet told us what you're going to call Charley. He's still a little boy, but you'll have to decide soon.'

'Charley will be styled Rockport – the Earl of Rockport, just as I was, and Father before me. I've always heard that Kilmourne, the Irish title, was unlucky – certainly it proved that for my brother – and besides that, we haven't much connection with Jordanstown now. Our place, and Charley's place, will be here in Mallamshire, and its right that he should bear a Mallamshire name.'

'Good,' said Lorna.

Rupert was smiling at his wife as she joined them; and Lorna felt a glow of satisfaction: the weather seemed set fair for the new Duke and his family as they prepared to take up their inheritance.

Three

The church of St Margaret in Antioch stood half-way up the village street in Rockport. It boasted a square tower with fine tracery windows that dominated the surrounding cottages; and it owed its unusual dedication to its founder, Sir Walter de la Noy, who had caused it to be built in the thirteenth century as a thank offering upon his safe return from a crusade. A dubious pedigree, damp-stained and fly-blown, that hangs in a back passage at Rockport Place, endeavours to link Sir Walter with his successors the Delaneys, who had acquired the Rockport lands after the dissolution of Mallaby Abbey; and the walls of the church and the lawns of the graveyard are filled with memorials to the forebears of the Delaney-Greys.

The church was not large, and it was filling steadily with family, friends and villagers. One side aisle was already packed: here sat both the tenant farmers and the estate workers, uncomfortable in their Sunday best. At the front were both the Lord Lieutenant and the High Sheriff, representing, as it were, Crown and County: the Mayors of Somersham and Shipston-upon-Mal, wearing their chains of office: and the presidents of various Mallamshire bodies who traditionally looked to the Dukes of Jordans for patronage; but in the main, the nave was ranked with ordinary folk anxious to join in the obsequies for the tenth Duke.

Dame Elizabeth de Blete had come over early from

Braye with her friends Lord and Lady Mallaby. Sitting upright in her pew as she looked around, the Dame had made a commanding sight: she was clad in a vast dusty black cape with a large rough metal clasp that made at least one onlooker think she more closely resembled an Albanian brigand than a distinguished retired civil servant. · Under an iron-grey bun, her face was weather-beaten and intelligent, now alight with curiosity as she turned to whisper to Angela Mallaby.

'I'm dying to see Sheila Jordans again. And I wonder how she's got herself up as the grieving widow.'

'She'll be here in a moment,' Angela Mallaby whispered back. 'Diana tells me that Colin is to escort her here. We'll have a chance to talk to Sheila over drinks at the big house afterwards.'

The Dame nodded, then smiled and half bowed to a friend, Lady Alice Brinscomb, who, as the late duke's sister, was on her way to the second pew from the front. There she joined his other sister, Lady Margaret Wright, who was already installed with her husband the colonel, her son Mark and his wife Jean.

Now Dame Elizabeth caught a glimpse of Canon Pew-Brown, hooded and robed, hovering by the door of the vestry.

'The canon says he's going to take the service briskly,' she murmured to Andrew Mallaby, 'the 1662 Prayer Book, of course, but no address. There's really very little to say about poor Jamey Jordans.'

The canon and the vicar of Rockport fluttered down the aisle in a sussuration of surplices, on their way to receive the widow. They passed Diana Jordans on her way to the front pew; alone, she looked very small, in a black tailored coat with a tiny cap perched on her neat dark hair.

The organist embarked on a portentous change of tune, and uneasily the congregation shambled to their feet. Then, forming a small procession and preceded by the verger bearing a high cross, the clergymen came back up the nave, followed by Sheila, with her hand in the arm of Rupert Jordans. The widowed duchess was short, almost dumpy: and despite the blackness of her shoes and stockings, gloves and handbag, despite the tailored simplicity of her black coat and skirt, there was about her an air of fluffy fussiness: a mauve angora was tucked around her neck; her face was elaborately made up in the fashion of the forties, with scarlet lips and arched eyebrows, and from under a hat of black veiling there crept wisps of white-blonde hair.

Behind Sheila and Rupert came Lord Colin: and what drew the attention of everyone was the woman on his arm. She was tall, swathed in a swaggering sable coat, with tawny hair falling in a pageboy bob across the glossy dark sheen of her fur collar. She had a broad, generous mouth like a gash across her strong-boned face, and her features were held solemnly, with deference to the occasion. She was wearing brown cossack boots that clicked on the stone flags as she marched up the nave, and the Dame, after a swift, calculating glance, guessed the stranger's age as the late thirties.

Angela Mallaby nudged her neighbour.

'Who on earth is that?' she whispered; and indeed the same question was in the minds of most of the congregation. But the Dame could only shrug, disconcerted that for once she didn't know the answer.

During the service, Dame Elizabeth set herself to remembering what she knew about Sheila Jordans. She had first met the fluffy little woman at Bishops Malford some nine years ago; she had then been Lady Fiske, the widow of an impoverished baronet with whom the Dame had a remote kinship. There had been a wayward son, Sir Joshua, the Dame recalled, but he had not been heard of since his mother attained her ambition and became Jamey Jordans' second duchess. What the Dame did not forget was the steely determination that lay beneath Sheila's fluttering femininity; and she hoped that Sheila's return to Mallamshire was not going to make waves for Rupert and Diana. With any luck, the widow would return to the Bahamas, and the waters could close over what had been an unhappy episode in the history of the Jordans family.

After the benediction, the congregation streamed out of God's blessing and into the warm autumn sunshine. Many crowded round Rupert and Diana, anxious to give their condolences, and although he was punctilious in introducing his stepmother, Sheila was generally ignored. Her friend stood on one side, watching but aloof. The Mallabys carried Dame Elizabeth off to their car, saying there would be time enough to talk at the big house.

At Rockport Place, the double doors between the great saloon and the green drawing-room had been opened; braided ropes, druggets, typed notes for visitors (stuck on to wooden bats) all tidied away. Log fires blazed in all four marble chimneypieces, and both Dobson and James stood ready with salvers of sherry and madeira to greet the company of mourners.

Dame Elizabeth drifted away, finding many Mallamshire friends whom she was glad to see. Soon, she brought up next to Lady Alice, and after an enquiry about her son Lord Brinscomb who had emigrated to Australia and was said to be doing well, with a baby boy to show for it, she decided to broach the subject of the stranger. After all, Alice had led a cosmopolitan life.

'Who is the woman who came in with Sheila? I couldn't imagine what she was doing in the family pew.'

Lady Alice was amused.

'My dear Dame E.,' she said, 'Do you mean to say you've never heard of Betty Bassano? What a sheltered life you've led, to be sure.'

The Dame looked blank, so Lady Alice explained.

Betty Bassano, she said, had been Betty Baker, of Baker's Margarines and Cooking Oils, a vast American corporation.

'I see,' said the Dame, 'big money, I take it?'

'Very big. When her first husband Ronnie Baker died, she copped the lot – no trust funds, no stepchildren, just two hundred million dollars.'

'Lucky Betty,' said the Dame. The sum involved was just too big for her to comprehend. 'I assume that she married again?'

'That's right. Ronnie Baker was a good deal older than Betty, and no one was surprised when, after he died, she became entangled with Paolo Bassano. He's one of those devastating Latin polo players, an absolute dish in sweatshirt and white jodhpurs – but not good husband material, my dear, if you know what I mean.'

Dame Elizabeth did know, although fortune-hunting polo players were not much in her line of country.

'The second marriage did not last, I take it?'

'A couple of years. Betty soon saw through him and bought him off. But she was a bit disillusioned with America after that, and I suspect that's why she has bought Lordstanding, to make a new life in England.'

'Ah,' said the Dame, with the air of one fitting the last piece into a jigsaw, 'so Mrs Bassano is the mysterious foreigner who took that lovely house. But why is Sheila Jordans under her wing?'

'Betty met Jamey and Sheila in Palm Beach, I think, and they became friends; so when Jamey died, it was natural for her to ask Sheila to stay.'

Dame Elizabeth nodded; then, looking over Lady Alice's shoulder, she spotted something odd going on. Mrs Bassano had strolled into a group made up of Lady Margaret Wright, her husband the colonel and her son Mark. After a few words, they all broke out into laughing and embracing and patting each other's shoulders, like the reunion of a long-parted family.

The Dame pointed at the group and remarked, 'It seems as if she knows your sister pretty well, too.'

Lady Alice's ravaged features broke into a grin. 'You've often said that all circles complete in Mallamshire,' she said, 'and there's an example. Betty is English by birth, you see: her family were quite modest, but her father served in the war with the colonel, who stood as her godfather; and he used to invite the little girl to Wrighton for the school holidays.'

'But how did she get to America?'

'... and lay her hands on Ronnie Baker and all those lovely dollars? I don't know, my dear, you'll have to find out for yourself. Why don't I take you two over to meet her?'

They moved through the assembly to join the Wrights, whom the Dame knew, and Betty Bassano was introduced.

'It's lovely to be back in Mallamshire, Dame Elizabeth,' Mrs Bassano said, 'and to meet up with old friends again. Are you Mallamshire too?'

'Not really,' said the Dame, 'I've only lived here since I retired. But that's nearly fifteen years, so I suppose they're beginning to accept me.'

'We couldn't get along without you, Dame E.,' said Lady Alice. She looked up at Betty. 'When anything goes wrong in the county, or when anyone's in trouble, it's always Dame Elizabeth who sorts out the mess.'

'I'll remember that, Dame Elizabeth,' Mrs Bassano drawled, 'and I hope you'll visit with me at Lordstanding.'

'That would be delightful,' the Dame responded. She was taking in the details of the stranger's appearance. Mrs Bassano was very tall, taller even than the Dame herself, who was beginning to shrink into the hump of age, and she had a good figure which she held well. The sables had been discarded, and she was wearing a very simple dress in grey jersey wool, beautifully cut and exactly right for the occasion. The voice was husky, well modulated, with the English overlaid by an American burr, and in the eyes was a droll, quizzical look that rather appealed to the Dame.

She would have liked further words with the stranger; but now Sheila Jordans irrupted into the group and, with a shriek of delight, flung herself against Dame Elizabeth.

'Dear Coz!' she cried. 'What heaven to see you again!'

The relationship had been remote – and through Sheila's first husband anyway – and the Dame was startled by the warmth of the greeting; but she made a suitable response and bent down to give the fluffy little woman a cousinly kiss.

While Sheila was bubbling away, explaining to Betty Bassano about the dear old days at Bishops Malford, Dame Elizabeth's attention was caught by the ring on her hand. It was a huge, square-cut emerald: and the last time she remembered seeing it, it was on the finger of the Dowager Duchess (Jamey's mother), *en grande tenue* for some great event. There was a family legend attached to the stone, and she was surprised to see it now on Sheila's hand at this quiet country gathering.

'… and Betty has been so kind, having me to stay at Lordstanding,' Sheila was saying.

'Do you plan to stay on for a bit?' the Dame asked, 'or will you go back to the Bahamas soon?'

'Betty has been most generous. She says I can stay as long as I like, and now I'm back in Mallamshire – where, after all, we belong – and among all my friends, I'm in no hurry to leave.'

Dame Elizabeth found herself thinking that although the Jordans belonged, Sheila certainly didn't: she had only lived in the county for a year or two before decamping with Jamey; and anyway, most of the company present were friends of Rupert and Diana rather than of the newly widowed Duchess; but she kept these thoughts to herself and answered civilly that she hoped Sheila would indeed extend her stay.

'Sheila's promised to keep me company until after Christmas, anyway,' Mrs Bassano put in. 'We're planning to have a real old English yuletide at Lordstanding.'

'And, dear coz, you simply must join us for that,' Sheila added. 'I'm expecting both my boys, and Betty has some most interesting people flying in from the States.'

Again the Dame accepted the general invitation in general terms. If a date was set, she would certainly accept; for one thing, she had a natural curiosity to see what all those dollars had done for Lordstanding, and for another, it would do no harm to keep an eye on Sheila Jordans. Dame Elizabeth had a nose for trouble: and she knew from experience just how much trouble Sheila could create. She would have been much happier had Sheila been departing for the Bahamas at once.

Brooding over what possible threat Sheila might represent, she glanced across the saloon. Both Rupert and Diana were circulating separately, making sure between them that everyone had time for a word. Dame Elizabeth was very fond of them both: standing by with advice and support, as their responsibilities had grown, as Rupert's name had changed from plain Delaney-Grey to Rockport and now to Duke.

The Dame had time for a few brief sympathetic sentences with Rupert before he was drawn into the circle gathered around Mrs Bassano, with whom, she noted, he was already on good terms; then she set off to find Diana, whom she detached from the clutches of the High Sheriff's wife.

'First, my dear, you must give my love to Lorna.'

Diana nodded. No more had to be said: both understood clearly that the Dame meant Rupert's mother to know that although she had been perfectly civil to Jamey's second duchess, her loyalty and affection lay with his first.

'Lorna's going to lie low,' Diana explained, 'just while Sheila plays the widow.'

'In that cases, she will be absent for a long time,' said the Dame. 'From what I've been told, Sheila intends to stay on at Lordstanding until after Christmas at the very least.'

'Two months more,' Diana sighed. 'She's very friendly, but she keeps trying to patronise me, which drives Rupert mad. And he's trying to have some business talk with her, but she simply won't come up with the answers he needs.' Diana lowered her voice to elaborate. 'Rupert is convinced that she has the Rockport rubies locked away somewhere: they don't belong to her, they couldn't because they're trust-bound, but Sheila is most evasive when pressed about their whereabouts.'

'Not only the rubies; did you see the ring on her claw-like finger?'

'The emerald? Yes, I did. I've never seen it before.'

'Well, I have,' the Dame stated firmly. 'The last time I saw it was on the occasion when Rockport Place was first opened to the public. Lorna laid on a tenants' dinner and the dowager, who was still very much alive then, was dressed in full fig. Among their heirlooms she displayed was that emerald.'

'You're sure it's an heirloom?' Diana asked, looking anxious. 'Its not something Rupert's father might have given Sheila?'

'It might be – but he had no right to. The dowager told me specifically that the ring belonged to the heirloom trust.'

'Then I'll have to warn Rupert.' Diana looked as if she wanted to say more, but Dobson now loomed up, bearing a salver of sherry decanters. Both ladies refused further refreshment, Diana with what the Dame considered an over-ingratiating effusion. When Dobson had given a stately half-bow and passed on his way, Diana put her hand on the Dame's arm.

'I have to admit Dobson scares the wits out of me,' she confessed. 'It's the one thing I'm dreading about our move into the big house.'

'Just be firm,' Dame Elizabeth advised. 'After all, you must have had plenty of experience of giving domestic orders in your father's hotel.'

'I know, but it's different here. Rupert and Colin don't understand, but they belong at Rockport Place – and so do Dobson and James the footman and that old dragon Aggie Smiles in the kitchen. Sometimes, I feel like an interloper. Neither Rupert nor I are formal people, and I can't get used to all this "Your Grace" business.'

The Dame wasn't particularly sympathetic; Diana was a lucky young woman to have well-trained domestic staff, and she was quite intelligent and forceful enough to form her own style as duchess. So she just patted Diana's hand and, after looking around and catching Andrew Mallaby's eye, said that they would have to be going.

On the way back to Braye, Dame Elizabeth, ensconced in the back of the Mallabys' car, felt an access of indignation.

'Three duchesses,' she snorted, 'it's quite ridiculous. I wish Sheila Jordans would pack her bags and go back to Nassau, or wherever she wants as long as it's well away from Mallamshire.'

Four

On a murky November evening, Rupert Jordans was driving over to Lordstanding. A dank mist lay in the river valley as he crossed the narrow stone bridge, and then he caught a glimpse of the lights of the house, gleaming yellow from the brow of the hill. He wasn't looking forward to his meeting with his stepmother, and nor, he gathered, was she; for weeks, she had prevaricated about setting a date, and each time he telephoned, she pleaded continuing grief or ill health. It was only when he spoke to Mrs Bassano, who proved unexpectedly helpful, that at last an appointment was made.

Rupert was alone. Diana was chairing a committee in Greyabbey and didn't expect to be back at Byegrove until late, which was just as well, he thought as he turned in at the drive gates, for he had no idea how long it would take to pin Sheila down to some concrete answers.

The door was opened by a white-coated manservant who led him through a broad hall hung with well-lit tapestries and into what was obviously a library. The room was empty and Rupert had time to take in his surroundings. One wall was lined with books, floor to ceiling (always a good sign), there was a vast desk, covered with papers, standing in a bay window whose tall windows were hung with swagged curtains in a strong yellow pattern. The same yellow appeared on deep sofas that were on either side of a blazing log fire; magazines were stacked on a sofa table, and all about there stood pots of white cyclamen and azaleas. It was a cheerful, friendly place on a chilly winter night, and Rupert felt comfortable at once.

'Hi there!' came a voice from the door, and Betty Bassano entered, in a bright red trouser-suit that enhanced her handsome tawny looks. 'Sheila will be down directly – meanwhile, let me fix you a drink.'

Rupert accepted a whisky and soda, with a generous portion of ice, and Betty gestured for him to sit down.

'I know you have to have a business talk with Sheila,' she said, 'but don't make it hard for her. She's had a tough time; she misses Jamey quite dreadfully, and his death was a fearful shock, for all she tries not to let it show. Your father was a very charming man, Rupert: we were all very fond of him.'

Now Sheila appeared, her hands extended and her cheek proffered for a kiss which Rupert rose to bestow. She was wearing a lilac coat and skirt, her ashen hair like a halo around her face. She too accepted a whisky and for a few moments they chatted inconsequentially, in the main about the improvements Betty had made to Lordstanding. During this, Rupert grew restive: he had screwed himself up to have things out with Sheila, and now was the opportunity.

'I know you'll forgive me, Betty,' he said, 'but I do have some financial matters to discuss with Sheila. Is there somewhere we might go to talk in private?'

'Stay here,' said Betty with a smile. 'I can easily make myself scarce.'

'No, no!' Sheila shrilled. 'Darling Betty is my dearest friend: whatever you have to say, you can say in front of her. There are no secrets between us.'

'Very well,' Rupert conceded reluctantly. If he needed to be firm, it might be embarrassing to have Betty sitting alongside his stepmother; but it was Betty's house and he had no choice. So he launched into an explanation of the provisions that were made for his father's widow, provisions that had been made by the trustees at the time of Sheila's marriage.

'But I know all this,' Sheila protested, interrupting, 'my beloved Jamey was most anxious that I shouldn't be worried about the future, if he should depart before me – as indeed he has.'

She heaved a sigh and looked so frail and sad that Betty leaned forward to pat her arm.

'H'm, yes,' said Rupert, hurrying on, 'well, there's no hurry, of course, but in due course the trustees will need to know your plans – where you plan to live, for instance.'

'Sheila's welcome to stay here as long as she likes – you know that,' Betty put in.

'Thank you, darling. It's too early, of course, to make up my mind yet, Rupert, but everyone's been so very sweet to me here in dear old Mallamshire that I'm beginning to think that perhaps I might like to come back for good.'

Rupert did his best to disguise the horror he felt at the idea.

'Just a little house in the country,' Sheila was saying brightly, 'and then maybe a tiny flat in town. It would enable me to see more of my boys, and darling Josh does need a mother's eye on him.'

Rupert's horror deepened: the thought of the wayward Sir Joshua as a permanent inhabitant of Mallamshire and as a member of the family circle was not one to cheer him up. And he was pretty sure that his stepmother's capital was insufficient for so expansive a way of life.

'You will have to go into all that with the trustees,' he temporised, 'and, as you know, I'm not one of them. I'm just here as an emissary.' He wanted to move on to tackle the question of the missing heirlooms.

'I'm sure they listen to what you say, Rupert dear,' Sheila said. 'And that reminds me: a little bird told me you and dear Diana are planning to move back into Rockport Place.'

'That's right,' he answered shortly. 'We hope to be settled by Christmas.'

'In that case' – her voice was elaborately casual – 'Byegrove will be empty?'

'Byegrove is different,' Rupert said very firmly indeed, 'it doesn't belong to any of the trusts.'

'Maybe not, but it's all in the family, isn't it?' Sheila gave him a shrewd look; her little eyes were suddenly hard.

'As I've said, where you live is a matter for the trustees and not for me; and, as you've said, you're in no hurry. What I have been asked to raise with you is the matter of some of the heirlooms. I have a list here of a number of items of jewellery which my father may have provided for you to wear while he was still alive. As I'm sure he must have made plain to you, such jewellery was not his property, and he had no power to make a gift of it. To put it simply, the heirlooms are and remain the property of a trust which provides them for the wife of the duke to wear.'

'Jamey was very generous,' said Sheila, her tone turning plaintive. 'He loved me to have pretty things, as what he called earnests of his love, bless him.'

'Will you have a look at the list?'

She waved it away. 'It wouldn't mean anything to me. Jamey looked after the insurance and all that.'

'Well,' Rupert pressed, 'I am sure you must remember the Rockport Rubies: they are made up into a necklace and matching ear-rings set in gold and embellished with diamonds. They are famous, and I'm sure Father must have told you about them.'

'It doesn't ring a bell.' Sheila shrugged. 'Jamey did

give me some rubies – they are my favourite stones – but I don't have them in England.'

'You must know where they are – they're very valuable.'

'Don't be such a fusspot, Rupert.' Sheila's face was beginning to flush. 'I simply don't know if I have what you call the Rockport Rubies or not. When I go back to Nassau, I'll have a look in the safe deposit: until then, you will just have to wait.'

Rupert glanced at his list. 'What about my Grandmama's emerald?'

'Now this is too much.' Sheila's mouth had dropped open and her eyes widened and were starting to glisten. 'That ring was given to me by my darling Jamey after his mother died and he said he wanted me to have it for always. And now ... now ...' she broke out with a sob, 'now, you want to strip it off my finger before the poor sweetie is cold in his grave.'

For a moment she buried her face in her hands; then, fumbling for a handkerchief and emitting a strangled whoop, she rose and scuttled for the door, which slammed shut behind her.

'Oh dear,' said Rupert, rising. His simian face was thin with distaste.

'Oh dear indeed,' Betty echoed, and Rupert turned to stare at her. He had forgotten the silent witness to that embarrassing scene.

'I really must apologise ...' he began.

'Oh, forget it, my dear man.' Betty gave him a friendly smile. 'Why don't I freshen up your drink? I expect you need it after all that.'

Gratefully, he handed over his glass, and Betty busied herself with the ice bucket.

'Mind you,' she drawled over her shoulder, 'I did my best to warn you. Sheila's nerves are still in very bad shape.'

'Will she come back, do you think?'

'No, she'll stay in her room. She needs a little privacy. I'll have something sent up to her later. Meanwhile, please make yourself comfortable and sit down again, just to show there are no hard feelings.'

Rupert subsided on to a sofa and Betty settled opposite, her long legs tucked up beneath her. With the log fire crackling and blazing between them, it was cosy, intimate even, and Rupert felt himself relaxing after the tension of facing up to his stepmother.

'I know you think I was rather tough on Sheila just now,' he said slowly, 'and I'm sorry. But she can't go on evading me for ever: I've got to have some answers.'

'Just why is this jewellery so important to you?' Betty asked.

'It's important that Sheila realises that it doesn't belong to her. It is all owned by a trust that was set up years ago, quite legitimately to avoid what were then called death duties; if Sheila insists on hanging on to property that isn't hers, or worse if she should start to sell the odd item, then the trustees will be put in an impossible position.'

'I can understand that,' Betty said, 'but you must see that from Sheila's point of view, you are asking her to hand over presents that Jamey gave her.'

'Yes, but he wasn't entitled to give them. If Sheila won't co-operate, then the trustees will have to take to the law. Their duty is not just to me, but to my son and his successors.'

'You wouldn't want to go to law,' said Betty flatly. 'The publicity would be horrible. In any case, there's nothing to stop Sheila whisking the jewels off to a bank in Miami: and I can't see an American court taking kindly to a rich stepson trying to strip his father's widow of her mite.'

'Some mite,' said Rupert grimly. 'The rubies alone are worth a king's ransom – not that that's the reason why I need them back.'

'Then why do you?' Betty's broad smile was encouraging, and Rupert found himself telling her about his discovery of the Carracci painting, and how he needed to have the Rockport Rubies assessed by an expert to complete the circle of his research.

'That's very exciting, I do see,' said Betty when he had finished. 'I will have to do what I can to persuade Sheila to make the stones available to your expert. But I can't promise anything: she can be very stubborn, you know, and although she's putting on a brave front, she's frightened for the future.'

'She has no need to be: as I've said, the trustees will make suitable provision for her.'

'I dare say.' Betty's smile was wry. 'But your trustees' idea of suitable provision and Sheila's may not coincide.'

They were interrupted by the entry of the manservant, to whom Betty gave orders for a tray to be taken to the duchess's room. Then she looked across at Rupert.

'I have an idea: why don't you stop over for dinner? Maria is a marvellous cook and it would be a pity to waste her efforts – besides, I hate having dinner alone. Do keep me company.'

Rupert hesitated. The house was warm and comfortable, this handsome woman was friendly and easy to talk to. And it would do no harm to have her on his side. Besides, outside it was a raw night, and Byegrove, already half dismantled against the impending move and with his wife absent in Greyabbey, would be empty and bleak.

'That would be delightful,' he said.

Dinner was set in a small square parlour that led off the library. It was a charming room, with pretty chintzes, bamboo chairs, and a round, flounced table. The dinner was delicious and served with dexterity; when the manservant was out of the room, Rupert told his hostess how fortunate she was on the domestic front.

'I suppose I am,' she conceded, 'I hadn't really thought about it. Pedro and Maria are Portuguese: they used to work for friends of mine in Jackson Hole, and when they heard I'd bought a house in England, they came and told me they wanted to return to Europe.'

'What on earth is Jackson Hole?'

'It's a small place in Wyoming, by the foothills of the Rockies. I have a ranch there.' She gave a laugh. 'Really, Rupert, you're so insular, for all you have an American mother. She would know exactly what Jackson Hole means.'

'And what is that?' Rupert was rather put out by her teasing.

'Roughly, it means you have to be a Du Pont or a Whitney or something approaching before you can be accepted in Jackson Hole.'

'I see – an enclave for the super-rich. And this is where your home was in the States.'

'One of them: I keep an apartment in Manhattan, of course; and there's the place in Palm Beach.'

'And now you've bought Lordstanding, you have four homes? Isn't that a bit confusing?'

'Not really. It's just a kind of circuit. My first husband Ronnie was locked into it when I married him: most of his friends revolved round it, with occasional diversions to Europe, and I just fell into it.'

'But you are English: how on earth did you come to meet your husband?' Rupert didn't feel diffident about such a direct question; the atmosphere was amiable and his curiosity was aroused.

'My mother died when I was eighteen, and my only living relative was an aunt who had married an American lawyer and gone to live in Los Angeles. They gave me a home.'

Betty made a good story of it: how she went out for a walk one afternoon (an unheard-of thing in California) and happened to encounter a stray spaniel; how a man in a huge black convertible drew up when she was looking for a dog's name-tab and accused the girl, gawky in jeans and shirt, of trying to steal it: she had answered back with spirit, telling him he should look after his animals better.

'Then, suddenly, we both laughed. He was tanned and silver-haired, and he had a lovely smile. In no time, we were friends: and six weeks later he asked me to marry him.'

'That was quick work,' said Rupert.

'Oh, I know, you're thinking what all Ronnie's friends thought − that I was just a gold-digger. But I honestly didn't know how rich he was: I just liked him enormously, and he made me feel safe as I'd never felt before. I realised − as my aunt said often enough − that Ronnie was old enough to be my father; but I loved him and he adored me, and we were happy together until the day he died.'

Betty fell silent, a shadow of sadness on her broad face.

'You must have been very lonely,' Rupert suggested quietly.

'I was,' she agreed, smiling at his understanding. 'Most of our friends were more Ronnie's age than mine; and although they were very kind to me, I couldn't help having the feeling that they wouldn't rest until they'd safely remarried me and all Ronnie's dollars to someone they considered suitable.'

'And that's what happened?'

'Not quite.' Betty looked rueful. 'Paolo Bassano was very attractive, and well known as a polo player. He's a great lover, too; but in no way is he responsible. Still, he seemed keen to marry me, and I was fool enough to think I could restrain his roving eye. I should have known better!' She laughed openly and without bitterness. 'I came back to my house in Palm Beach one afternoon, unexpectedly, and found that rat Bassano in

bed with my best friend. She was twenty years older
than me, which made it worse. Anyway, I just threw him
out.'

'And you're divorced now?'

'Yes, I am. It was tough, and it cost me plenty, but I
got rid of him in the end. It was about then that I
became friends with Jamey and Sheila. We'd met at the
Polo Club, and we took to each other. I suppose all
being English, and exiles, helped. Anyway, Sheila was a
real chum during the divorce, and I needed chums
then: I'd rather lost caste with the Jackson Hole circuit,
and was becoming fed up with America anyway.'

Betty broke off to take a sip of her wine, and Rupert
looked at her appraisingly. He liked her frankness, and
her common sense; there weren't many women he knew
who would be so downright about a mistaken marriage.
Suddenly, he was glad that she had been a friend of his
father in exile.

'So you decided to come back to England: but why
Mallamshire?'

'I had happy memories of this part of the country,
from the times when I used to stay at Wrighton for the
holidays. Your aunt and uncle were very kind to me: so
when Sheila lent me a copy of *Country Life* and I saw this
house was for sale, I decided to buy it.'

'Just like that? Without even looking at it?'

'Well, I had seen it from the outside, when I used to
ride past with the pony club; and I used to dream that
one day I would live here. So I just called my attorney
and my bankers and told them to go ahead with the
purchase.'

'That's American hustle for you,' said Rupert.

Now, with dinner over, they returned to the library,
where the coffee had been set on a table in front of the
sofa. The fire was blazing with fresh logs, the flames
glinting on the leather spines of the book-lined walls;
with the scent from the pots of flowers and the soft

lamps it felt like a luxurious sanctuary, a feeling emphasised by a squall of rain outside that spattered against the window panes. They sat down side by side, Betty once more curling up in her corner.

'Tell me about your sons,' she suggested. It was time, she felt, that Rupert was encouraged to talk about himself.

'Charley and Jonathan?' He smiled. 'There's really nothing to say. They're just rather nice, ordinary little boys. Mind you, it's odd to think that one day Charley will be duke in my place: it takes a little getting used to.'

'Have you got used to it? Being duke, I mean.'

'Strangely enough, yes. I suppose I've been running the estate for long enough, and with my father abroad, Diana and I have been doing all the dukely things around the county, so it hasn't made much difference. It was a far worse shock when my elder brother died, and without warning I found myself heir in line.' He was going on to say that he could not have coped without Diana at his side but stopped: it didn't seem the right remark at the time.

'When you come to think about it,' Betty was saying, 'it's a fairly absurd word, isn't it? Duke, I mean.'

'Any word becomes absurd when you repeat it. And I suppose it's a fairly absurd thing to be, in this day and age. It's a pretty ridiculous system that entails my changing my name three times: even little Charley at the age of seven is having to get used to calling himself something else. Still, absurd or not, one has to do the job as best one can. And it does mean something here in Mallamshire.'

'Of course it does,' Betty agreed firmly. 'It's all part of the English tradition. And that's one of the reasons why I'm so happy to be back.'

'And I hope you're going to stay, and not go gallivanting off on that circuit all round America.' Rupert smiled along the sofa.

'Before I make up my mind, I'm going to give it a full year here at Lordstanding. Then we'll see.' She gave him a steady look, to see if he was ready for a confidence, and decided that he was.

'I have a confession,' she began. 'When I saw the picture of Lordstanding and the idea formed in my mind to come here, there was at the back of it a faint hope that I might meet up with Mark again. The Wrights had been so good to me, and Mark was always very sweet, never resenting the ungainly schoolgirl he'd been landed with: my dream was that we'd fall in love, be married and settle to have a large family.' She made a rueful moue at her own idiocy and they both laughed.

'You're about three years too late,' Rupert told her, 'and I think Mark and Jean are very happy together.'

'Indeed they are – and Jean's a delightful woman. But I do want to have children, and time is not on my side.'

'Don't be so morbid, Betty, you don't look a day over twenty-five.'

'That's very sweet of you, my dear, but I have to face the fact that I'm not far off forty. It was a sadness for both Ronnie and for me that we never had children.'

'What about your polo-player?'

Betty shook her head firmly. 'It didn't take many months of marriage to Paolo for me to see that it would be madness to inflict a litter of half-Bassanos upon the world. Still, I've been fortunate in other ways: I'd do best to count my blessings.'

With a shake of her head, as if to dismiss her thoughts, Betty now rose, going over to fix them both a whisky. Settled again, their talk turned to other, and increasingly intimate, topics. What with one thing and another, it was very late indeed when Rupert found himself driving home through the black night to Byegrove.

Five

'Stir up, we beseech thee ...' With just such a brisk
invocation, Diana Jordans found herself remembering
every year, began the collect for the Sunday Next
Before Advent. Traditionally, it also served to remind
the housewives in the congregation to see to their
Christmas puddings: nowadays, it marked the appearance of the lists. For those who have to organise the
festive season, the lists are vital: lists of food and drink,
lists of recipients for cards, lists for parties, lists of
Christmas tips, lists of presents. The list of lists seemed
endless, and this year for Diana they were multiplied by
the imminent move of her household from the
accustomed comfort of Byegrove to the unknown
territory of Rockport Place.

Diana was efficient, and knew her capabilities; but she
realised her limits. Together with Jean Wright, she went
through her diary, endeavouring to give herself a clear
two months without public duties. Even so, there were
some fixtures, events dear to her heart which she
refused to cancel, such as opening the annual fair of arts
and crafts in Somersham: the organisers, hitherto
content with the countess, were looking forward to
being opened by the new duchess, and such as these she
did not disappoint.

So, on the day after Stir-Up Sunday, Diana found
herself alone in the Dutch parlour in the big house. All
around was the evidence of builders' activity – trestles

51

and saws, ladders and planks, an electric kettle and some dirty mugs sitting incongruously on the marble hearth. But there was progress: bare wires poked out of the panelling showed the electricians had done their bit, and with a little imagination Diana could imagine the room as it would be when the family collection of Dutch seascapes were back on the walls.

The Dutch parlour took its name not from the paintings but from a fine collection of Delft. This had been reassembled for display by Rupert: remembering a chance remark of his grandfather's, that some fine pieces had been a present to the first duke from his uncle Wiliam of Orange, he had hunted them all down: one jar had been suffering the indignity of service as an umbrella stand in the cloakroom at the Dower House, another had been acting as a door-stopper in a little-used bedroom, a huge platter was discovered on the dresser in Aggie Smiles's kitchen. All were, miraculously, undamaged. Diana had decided not to replace them in the parlour, where they might be in danger from children; instead, they were to form a new feature in the vestibule to the great hall, under a portrait of King William himself.

Thinking of Rupert, Diana reminded herself that they were due to meet at his mother's house for lunch. She was glad of this: they had both been so busy recently that they had seen little of each other: Rupert was pre-occupied with problems on the estate and with the trustees. In spite of several visits to Lordstanding, he did not appear to have made much progress with his stepmother, and there was still no news of the Rockport Rubies. Diana had a feeling that Rupert was dragging his feet over the business but she did not press him: she wouldn't want him – or anyone else – to think that she was over-anxious to secure the missing jewels for her own adornment.

Diana tried to force herself to concentrate on the job

in hand, working out where the furniture was to go when the parlour became her own sitting-room, but she was distracted by a sullen, doom-like feeling of dread in the pit of her stomach. Today was the day appointed when she had arranged to introduce her own, much-loved housekeeper, Molly Platt, to the old guard in the servants' hall. That this meeting went well was important for the future smooth running of Rockport Place, and she just hoped that Dobson wouldn't scare the wits out of Molly.

Molly was an old friend. Diana had first known her when she was a waitress in the restaurant at her father's pub. Molly had then eloped with the chef, who soon abandoned her and their love-child: it had been Dame Elizabeth who secured Molly's return to Mallamshire and found her a position as barmaid in her own local. Later, when Diana was expecting her first baby, the dame had suggested Molly as a potential nanny, and that had proved a great success, Molly and her son Elvis becoming part of the growing family at Byegrove. Molly herself proved capable – and, what was just as important, always cheerful; as Diana's duties grew, Molly had gradually taken over the running of the household, seeing to the kitchen, keeping a watchful eye on the nursery, yet willing to do anything that might make for the greater comfort and wellbeing of her mistress. In short, without Molly, Diana's life would be impossible.

'Oh, Miss Diana!' came a broad, excited voice from the door, 'them new kitchens are a dream, really they are.' Molly Platt came in, her large shining face beaming with enthusiasm. She was a tall, full-figured woman with strong bones and a vast bosom. 'And the nurseries too. At first I was quite put out at the thought of leaving Byegrove, but now I'm all excited. I think we're all going to be very happy here in the big house, for all that it's not quite what you might call cosy.'

'I hope you're right, Molly,' Diana smiled back, 'But we have a great deal of work to do before we'll be comfortable. And now I think it's time we headed for the servants' hall. I'll introduce you, then leave you all to make friends.' Diana was forcing herself to sound more cheerful than she felt, and the feeling of doom became more leaden as they crossed the great hall, passed through a green baize door and went down a vaulted, stone-flagged corridor painted in thick cream with clusters of huge pipes running along near the ceiling. Then they descended some stone steps to face a door.

'Here we go,' said Diana, betraying her nervousness with a thin quick smile. She almost felt she should knock; instead, she took a deep breath and walked in.

'Good morning everybody,' she said breezily, 'I've brought Molly Platt in to meet you all.'

The room was warm and fuggy, with steam rising from a kettle standing on the hob of the long double Aga. It smelled faintly of fried bacon, with undertones of stewed tea, toast, and a faint aroma of silver polish.

'Good morning, Your Grace,' Dobson intoned, bending slightly at the waist. He was standing by the table, looming enormous, his beetling eyebrows like tuffets of heather surmounting a craggy cliff. Diana led Molly up to him and they shook hands, which Dobson made into a ceremony.

Then Diana went over to Aggie Smiles, who, after making a sketchy attempt to rise from her rocking-chair drawn up beside the range, had subsided again into a cocoon of knitted shawls, the chair still rocking as she held out a gnarled hand.

'How do you do, Mrs Platt,' she croaked, 'pleased to meet you, I'm sure.'

The screwed-up face held a glint of malevolence that belied the greeting, and Diana hurried on to introduce James the footman, who was hovering, so bent that it was difficult to tell if he was standing or sitting, by the door to the pantry.

'Mrs Smiles and I,' Dobson was pronouncing, 'generally take a cup of tea and some cake at this hour. Mrs Platt might care to join us?'

'What a good idea,' said Diana brightly, as if she hadn't planned the occasion, 'I know Molly is longing to hear from you all how the place used to be run in the old days.'

Having thus set what she hoped would be the direction of their converse, Diana thankfully escaped upstairs into the brighter light where Jean Wright's office could be found.

Jean got up from her desk as soon as Diana came in. She was tall, much taller than Diana, and with her dark hair cut short and her severe spectacles, she looked very much the efficient secretary, which she was. But she was more: since she had come to work at Rockport Place, she had gathered into her competent hands much of the administration, besides attending to the correspond-ence of the duke and duchess and maintaining their crowded diaries. It was understood that when the time came for the comptroller Tom de Blete (brother to the Dame) to retire, Jean would take his place, assuming control of the enterprise that promoted to the public the attractions of the great house. This understanding Jean's marriage to Rupert's cousin Mark had done nothing to diminish.

Jean suggested coffee.

'You look as though you need it,' she said. 'I suppose you've left Molly in the lion's den?'

Diana nodded. 'I must say it's very cosy down there: I just hope they won't make poor Molly feel unwelcome.'

'They do themselves very well in the servants' hall,' Jean agreed. All the accounts for provisions passed across her desk. 'They must eat about five meals a day – they can't have time for much else.'

'Well, we mustn't grudge them their comfort in their

old age: they've served the family well and now we must look after them.'

To take her mind off what might be happening downstairs, Diana asked to see the diaries. There was nothing inquisitive about this: she found it useful to see what were Rupert's engagements, so she would have some idea of his activities when they were together and exchanging news. It was Jean's custom to pencil in Rupert's movements as she knew of them, mainly for her own use, and Diana noticed several entries that read simply 'Lordstanding.'

'I wish I could believe that Rupert was making some progress over the rubies,' she remarked. 'But I have the feeling that Sheila is keeping him on a hook. He says he's hoping to get that friend of hers – Mrs Bassano – on his side.'

'Betty Bassano? She's a good sort and the greatest fun,' said Jean. 'Mark and I were over there for dinner last night and she gave us a lovely time.'

'Indeed? I'm sure she did. Of course, Mark knew her when she was a girl,' Diana reminded herself. 'For myself, I only met her briefly after the memorial service, but I liked the little I saw. Tell me, did Sheila give any clues about returning to the Bahamas?'

'Not a sign: if you ask me, she's dug in for the winter.'

'More's the pity,' came a new, male voice from the door. Tom de Blete, scenting coffee and chat, had joined them. He was a round little man, quite unlike his imposing sister, with a bald pate and a curious yellow complexion, gained, Diana had always assumed, by a kind of osmosis from his many years in the Far East.

'What have you against Sheila?' asked Diana. 'I thought she used to be very friendly with you and Phoebe.'

'That's just it,' said Tom. 'When we all lived in Bishops Malford, she was always in and out of our house. She was only a baronet's widow and down on her luck then: now she's a duchess, she's become a stuck-up little bitch.'

'Why, Tom, what on earth did she do?' It was unlike the comptroller, Diana thought, to be so venomous.

Tom explained that on the preceding Thursday, his wife had gone to London for some shopping.

'Phoebe was in the book department at Harrods when she happened to spot Sheila, wrapped in a huge fur coat, passing down the aisle. Naturally she went over to say hello. But Sheila cut her stone dead – looked through poor Phoebe as though she was an impertinent stranger and headed into a lift.'

While Tom was telling this story Jean, very casually, reached down for Rupert's diary, which still lay open on Diana's lap, closed it and replaced it on her desk. Quick thinking was another of her attributes, and Diana, engrossed in Sheila's odd behaviour, had not noticed:

They were distracted by the entry of Molly Platt who came in and stood by the door, her shining face very red.

'My goodness, Miss Diana,' she said, 'they're a stuffy lot down there and no mistake.'

'But how did you get on, Molly?'

'Oh, they're that pompous, Miss Diana, you wouldn't credit it. They call each other "Mr Dobson" and "Mrs Smiles", and insisted on me being "Mrs Platt", even though I explained I wasn't wed. They'd heard about my little Elvis, you see – not that I'm ashamed of him, the love.'

'I know you're not, Molly,' Diana assured her.

'Then they started in at me, because I call you Miss Diana, Miss Diana – told me it was all wrong and I'd have to get used to "Your Grace" like everyone else in my station.'

'That's rubbish, Molly. I've told you – you and I are good friends and you must call me whatever you like. What else did they have to say?'

'They asked me all sorts of questions. Like how many housemaids we were going to have. I told them, Miss Diana, that we weren't going to have no housemaids, even if such things exist these days which I doubt, and that we'd make do with ladies from the village to help us, just as we always have.'

'That's a relief,' Diana smiled. 'It's sad, really, that they still think in pre-war terms.'

'Don't you believe it,' Molly returned robustly. 'Mr Dobson explained to me that he expected he would need at least two more footmen, and a boy to help with the silver.'

'Good gracious, it's out of the question.' Diana sounded very firm indeed. 'Apart from the fact that what sounds like a royal household is not my style – and nor is it Rupert's – we could never afford it, could we, Tom?'

'Domestic staff are not my province,' he said, disclaiming responsibility. 'but I'm certain such additional servants would prove a considerable strain on your resources.'

'It's not only Mr Dobson,' Molly went on, 'it's Mrs Smiles too. She told me she would insist on having a scullery maid to fetch and carry for her, and extra hands for a big dinner party; and she more or less hinted that she'd expect me to help out as well. It's too much, Miss Diana,' Molly's face looked strained as she stared straight ahead of her. 'In fact, I'm beginning to think it's a mistake for me to move in here at all. Maybe it would be better if I cleared off and left you and his Lordship – I mean His Grace – now you've become duke and duchess.'

'Molly, you must not even think like that.' Diana was aghast. 'You will be in charge of our household, just as you are at Byegrove. You need have nothing to do with Dobson or Mrs Smiles. When I have time, I'll have a word with them both and put them straight.'

'Not before time, I'd say,' said Jean, who had several times suffered belittlement before Dobson's eyebrows.

'Unfortunately, I'm due at the Dower House soon, so I'll have to leave it for the moment.' Diana was aware that she was glad of the excuse to postpone the confrontation. 'After lunch,' she went on, 'I'll drive back with my husband so you'd better take my car home.'

She handed over her keys to Molly, who took them as ceremoniously as if they were emblems of office and, her face cleared, left the room.

'I'm going to hatch Christmas plans with Lorna,' Diana said, 'and that reminds me: although we won't do much here, for we'll only just have moved in, we are hoping that a few friends will come in for drinks after church on Christmas Day. You and Phoebe will join us, won't you, Tom: and of course, Jean and Mark too?'

Tom de Blete accepted at once, but Jean shook her head.

'I'm afraid we won't be able to make it,' she said, 'We will be expected at Wrighton, and the colonel would be awfully upset if we weren't there.'

'I quite understand. Anyway,' Diana proceeded happily, 'we are bound to see each other at the Mallabys' on Boxing Day.'

'Mark and I won't be there either.'

'My dear Jean, why not? We always go to Braye on Boxing Day, it's almost a tradition by now, and Angela and Andrew will be most upset if you don't turn up.'

Jean looked uncomfortable.

'We haven't actually been invited by Angela yet,' she began to explain.

'You don't need inviting – they're not formal – you just go.'

'Not this year, I'm afraid. As we hadn't heard from Angela, we've accepted another invitation. Betty Bassano is planning a big do at Lordstanding on Boxing Day: she has a full house party, and both the Lucktons and the Brinscombs are going so it sounds like fun.'

'I see.' Diana said no more, but began to assemble her scarf and bag, and then set out for the short walk across the park to the Dower House. This Mrs Bassano, she was thinking, was making great social headway for a newcomer; both the Lucktons and the Brinscombs were part of a well-heeled, well-connected set in their thirties: both wives were by birth foreign, Lady Luckton being a Latin American of great beauty and Caro Brinscomb an Australian. Still, they were both members of old Mallamshire families and, Diana concluded, if Betty Bassano had social aspirations, it did her no harm that she had under her roof, as what was beginning to look like a permanent house guest, Sheila Duchess of Jordans.

As she breasted the hill and approached the porch of the Dower House, she decided herself to ask the two couples to Rockport on Christmas morning. They would have to be invited some time anyway, and they were sure to be curious to see the big house now it was again a family home. She knew that deep down this was less a gesture of hospitality than an obscure one in the eye for Mrs Bassano, who seemed to crop up everywhere these days, but what the hell, she thought, as she pushed open the door and entered the morning-room.

This room, though empty, was bright and comfortable. A log fire smouldered in the basket grate and a bowl of forced yellow narcissus brought a waft of spring into the air. Diana had seen Rupert's car at the side so, wondering where he was, she went over to the deep bay window whose ogival casements overlooked a lawn running down to a ha-ha that divided it from the park.

Rupert and his mother were standing side by side, examining a catalpa tree so bent and crooked that its black limbs seemed to run along the grass like sea-serpents. Diana smiled as she watched: Lorna had been pursuing the estate office for months, trying to arrange for some crutches for the tree's aged limbs, and now she was pinning Rupert down to attend to it.

When they joined Diana, their faces were chilled by the wind, and Lorna's ashen hair was tousled and blown. She asked why Diana hadn't fixed herself a drink and set to remedy the deficiency while Diana, glad to see her husband (for they were both so busy they seldom had much time together), clung to his arm and lifted her heart-shaped face to kiss his icy cheek.

They were soon engrossed in Christmas plans. Lorna offered to provide lunch on the day itself, after the drinks at the big house: it would take the strain off Diana's untried kitchen.

'That's splendid,' Diana accepted, 'and it all means there'll be no question of that horrid Mrs Smiles trying to horn in. I suppose I'll have to ask Dobson and James to help with the drinks.' Her face clouded, and Rupert laughed.

'I can't see why you're in such a dither about that lot below stairs,' he said. 'Old Dobson would be mortified if you didn't rope him in.'

'It's all very well for you,' she retorted, 'you don't have to face up to his terrifying eyebrows.'

Lorna had seen the shadow in Diana's eyes.

'I suppose the old boy can be a bit intimidating,' she agreed. 'Never having lived in the big house, thank God, I haven't had much to do with the staff. Anyway,' she went on, changing the subject, 'who are you going to ask?'

'Just the family, and the usual crowd, plus some neighbours. And I thought we'd add the Lucktons and the Brinscombs.'

'The list seems to be growing, as party lists always do,' said Rupert, 'so why don't we throw in Betty Bassano? She's been very nice to me whenever I've been over to Lordstanding to talk sense into Sheila, and I want to keep her on my side.'

Lorna looked startled, but said nothing: Diana, however, weighed in at once.

'Rupert, it's out of the question. She has Sheila staying, and a whole host of Americans, and she'd have to ask if she could bring them all. We're just having a small family party with a few friends, and I wouldn't want your mother to come face to face with Sheila under our roof.'

'I suppose you're right,' Rupert grudgingly conceded, 'but perhaps we could suggest she came on her own.'

'I wouldn't do that. For one thing, we don't know her well enough; and for another, we can't ask her to abandon her house party during Christmas.'

'Oh well. At least we can go to her party on Boxing Day,' said Rupert, brightening up.

'Boxing Day?' Diana's voice rose. 'But we always go to the Mallabys' on Boxing Day.' She was beginning to think that this Mrs Bassano was looming too large in her life.

'I know,' said Rupert, 'but there's nothing to stop us looking in at Braye and then going on to Lordstanding. From what I've been told, Betty's do will go on for some time and she's laying on a buffet lunch.'

'Well, we'll see.' Diana didn't want to argue further in front of Rupert's mother; but privately she determined to arrange that something would prevent their attendance at Mrs Bassano's party.

When they had moved into the dining-room, and while Lorna's Filipino maid was handing round a steaming shrimp pilaff, Lorna asked Rupert how his research was going, and had he yet established a link between the Carracci painting and the rubies.

'I've had a bit of luck,' he said. 'I thought I might have to wait until the wretched Sheila coughed up the necklace, but I discovered that the trustees had some photographs of the jewels, taken for insurance purposes. After Christmas I might well take them over to Holland myself and have a talk with the experts.'

'I've never been to Amsterdam,' said Diana, 'and I

would love to see the Ryksmuseum. Perhaps I'll come along with you, darling.'

'Perhaps,' said Rupert: and he too added the indefinite prevarication, 'We'll see.'

Six

There is a sameness about Christmas which those who love it call tradition, and which those who hate it dismiss as a bore. Diana Jordans had heard the stories of the old days, when Rupert's grandfather had insisted on a complete turn-out of the whole family, down to the remotest cousin and the most infirm aunt, at his table: when a soaring Christmas tree was brought in from the estate and erected in the great hall, decked with candles and bells and with a footman posted, bucket and pump beside him, whenever the tree was lit in case it caught fire.

This year, her first in the big house, Diana was determined to do things well, albeit on a more modest scale. The tree was already in place in the library, and Molly Platt had decorated it charmingly all in silver, with a myriad little green electric lights. As for Diana's party, it had grown, as parties always do: the vicar and his wife could not be forgotten, nor could the agent and his live-in girl friend, and they were certain to see more eager faces after church. They had better allow for at least thirty people to drinks, she decided, and that would mean more hands. So, a week before the day, she nerved herself to leave the sanctuary of the Dutch parlour and go to seek out Dobson.

The butler was in his pantry, a snug retreat off a passage beyond Aggie Smiles's kitchen. A heaped coal fire blazed in the grate, and beside a comfortable leather armchair were *The Times* and *The Mallamshire Gazette,* neatly folded. Dobson himself, with a green apron around his ample waist, was seated at a table in the middle of the room which was heaped with stacks of silver-gilt – not only forks and spoons in serried ranks but epergnes and coasters, cruets, wine-coolers and an elaborately wrought centre-piece in the shape of two rams. There was a heavy, bitter smell of silver polish in the air and Diana, her eyes widening as she looked down at the display, felt it was more like a bank vault than an antiquated domestic office.

'Good morning, Your Grace,' said Dobson, his eyebrows raised in surprise at the intrusion. Unhurriedly, he moved to the door, removed his apron and put on a black coat. 'If Your Grace had cared to ring, I would have attended immediately.'

'Of course Dobson: I just thought it was easier to come and see you.'

The eyebrows quivered a reprimand: consideration was not expected of the chatelaine of Rockport Place.

'Anyway,' Diana went on, ignoring the eyebrows, 'I wanted to have a word about the Christmas plans.'

'Certainly, Your Grace,' Dobson intoned, 'and in anticipation of the festive season, I have ventured to withdraw the Paul Storr service from the strong-room to prepare it for use.' He bowed towards the laden table. 'It was His late Grace who always insisted on the Paul Storr being used at Christmas. He used to remark that there was little point in our possessing such beautiful objects if we didn't employ them as their maker intended.'

'Well, I'm sorry, Dobson, but we won't have a chance to use it all this Christmas. I've already made it clear that we are having luncheon at the Dower House. However, I am going to need your help on Christmas morning.'

'Indeed, Your Grace?' Dobson, rebuffed, retreated into impassivity.

'Yes: we're having a few friends in for drinks after church – nothing formal, you understand, but I hope you and James will serve. Rupert – I mean, His Grace – asked me to tell you to bring up the Bollinger.'

Dobson bowed his acknowledgement and Diana hurried on.

'Molly will be making a batch of her vol-au-vents – she's famous for them – but she'll have to keep an eye on the boys so I wondered if James might hand them round.'

'I will instruct him, Your Grace. And if I might suggest it, Mrs Smiles is famous for her cheese straws.'

'Of course, Dobson, we'll have them as well.'

Diana made her escape, relieved that the interview had gone so well.

Christmas itself began before dawn. Diana awoke suddenly, aroused by a noise. The window-panes were still black with night; peering across her bedroom she could just see, hovering by the open door, a pale shadow. It was her son Jonathan, one starfish hand clutching at the stocking as tall as himself, the other clasping his pyjama bottoms.

'Jonathan, you little goose!' she hissed across at him. 'It's too early, go back to bed, before your freeze to death.'

'But Mummy, I am cold,' he pleaded, 'and it is Christmas now, isn't it?'

'Oh, very well.' She gave in and lifted up the covers. 'Hop in here beside me and get warm.'

The little boy shot across the room and into her bed, his bumpy stocking scraping her leg as he snuggled down alongside her. He was very still, and for a few moments Diana dared to hope she might drop off to sleep again; but soon there was another voice, a sharper treble, and now it was Charley.

'Happy Christmas, Mummy!' he piped. 'I heard Johnnie was up so I knew you'd be awake.'

'I'm not,' she said firmly, her eyes shut. But she knew he too had come across the room and was staring into her face.

'See if you can creep in between me and Daddy,' she whispered, 'but mind, not a sound until Daddy wakes up.'

It was too late: Rupert's tousled head had emerged from his pillow. With the two boys bouncing on their bed, there was nothing for it but to turn on the lights and admit that Christmas had definitely begun.

With her family all around her on the bed, Diana felt a deep sense of completeness. Here they were together, the three she loved most in the world, with the world itself shut out beyond the closed windows. With a sigh of contentment, she tucked her arm into Rupert's and side by side they watched as their sons investigated their stockings. Jonathan's chubby fingers pulled out all the little presents at once, spilling them over the eiderdown: then he selected the one he liked best, two plastic green frogs in a snowstorm that whirled when you shook it, and this he began to study with concentration. Charley, meanwhile, after examining each package with care, settled happily to dismantling an old clockwork alarm which Diana had found in a forgotten cupboard and put in his stocking as a last-minute addition.

It was a rare moment of serenity in their busy lives. Diana had been so pre-occupied, both with the move and with the run-up to Christmas, that she had had little time to spend with the boys; and Rupert himself was concerned with major decisions for the estate's future, besides his worry about chasing Sheila for the missing heirlooms, that days had passed when they hardly saw each other. But, apart from their own small party and the trip to Braye, they had Christmas to themselve and their boys, and Diana was looking forward to it all with a glow of happiness.

Later that morning, people began to straggle across

the park to Rockport Place from the church. They bore that shriven look of wellbeing that comes from attendance at the Church of England at its traditional best and from an obligation discharged, together with an eager anticipation at the chance to see the new duke and duchess at home.

Dobson had posted James the footman at the side door, to relieve the guests of their hats and coats, scarves and gloves. He himself took up station at the double doors that led into the library where Rupert and Diana stood ready to receive, having struck their usual bet between themselves as to who would be first to arrive. They didn't have long to see: Dobson straightened himself, tucked a salver under his arm and, eyebrows signalling, trumpeted in a mighty voice.

'Major-General and Mrs Makepeace!'

'I've won!' Diana nudged Rupert. 'But,' she added, frowning, 'I do wish Dobson wouldn't do that. I told him we weren't being formal – you have a word with him, darling.'

'Oh, let the old boy have his head,' Rupert whispered back. 'He's enjoying himself and it is Christmas.'

They were now busy greeting the general and his wife, who had lately taken a lease of a large thatched cottage at the far end of Rockport village's only street; and soon the room was full of friends, neighbours and relations, pink with goodwill and Dobson's second-best champagne. The two little boys in scarlet pullovers, released from the nurseries by Molly Platt who stood watchfully by the door into the conservatory, were in tearing high spirits as they ran in and out of the legs of the guests.

Dame Elizabeth de Blete found herself next to Rupert.

'It's good to see Rockport Place as a family house again,' she told him. 'It must have been a wrench to leave Bye-grove, but I hope you will all be very happy here.'

'Thank you, Dame E.,' he grinned at her. 'Mind you, it isn't all plain sailing. I have a lot of hard decisions to make about the estate.'

'Quota trouble?' the Dame asked sympathetically.

'That, of course,' said Rupert, 'but the shoot is losing money, our takings from visitors are well down, and the forestry won't yield a penny until young Charley is in his forties. I'm thinking of going into deer-farming,' he added gloomily, 'and I've been approached by a syndicate that wants to turn the home park into a golf course.'

'Heaven forbid,' said the Dame with vigour.

'I know, dreadfully surburban. But it would yield more than farmland does.'

The Dame looked more closely at her host. She was devoted to Rupert and they had been close friends since the days when he was courting Diana. Now, he seemed taut, nervy, which was unlike him.

'These difficulties on the estate aren't new to you,' she pointed out, 'and the great thing in life is to be presented with problems you know you can solve. I'm sure you'll make the right decisions, both for the estate and for the future.' It occurred to her that something else might be worrying him, and decided to probe.

'Is Sheila making waves? And have you made any progress in retrieving the Rockport Rubies?'

She noticed that Rupert seemed to stiffen as she spoke; perhaps she had touched on the problem, so she went on.

'If you ask me, the best thing you can do is leave the whole matter in the hands of your trustees. It may well lead to some embarrassment if you get involved in a row with your stepmother.'

'My dear Dame Elizabeth,' Rupert said very formally indeed, 'when I am in need of your advice, I will ask for it.'

With that, he turned and left her. Astonishment on

her face, she watched his retreating back. She wasn't hurt, she told herself, by his curt rebuff; but she was very, very surprised: it was quite unlike Rupert to pull rank.

'Well, well, Bessie,' came a familiar voice from behind her, 'you look as if you've had a slap on the belly from a wet fish!'

She spun round and saw it was her brother Tom.

'Rupert is behaving in the most peculiar way,' she explained.

'I'm not surprised,' said Tom. 'If you ask me, there's trouble brewing in that quarter.'

'What do you mean?' The Dame, ignoring his opening vulgarity (to which she was well accustomed), pounced.

Tom, knowing his sister's appetite for news, looked round to make sure that, in the crowd, they were not overhead; then he began to tell her about his wife's visit to Harrod's and how she had been cut by Sheila.

'Ah,' said the Dame, 'just as I feared: what we used to call Bubbles trouble.'

'Bubbles' was the war-time nickname that Sheila Jordans had resurrected when she took up with Jamey.

'Not exactly, though I suspect she's encouraging Rupert. You see, after I had told Diana and Jean Wright about Sheila's behaviour, I happened to notice that Jean performed a very deft act in closing Rupert's diary and putting it away.'

'Tom, I hope you're not going to tell me you've been sneaking a look at other people's diaries. That's just not done.' Dame Elizabeth sounded as bossy as she had done in their nursery fifty years ago.

'It's not like that, Bessie. Neither Rupert's diary nor Diana's are private: they are just engagement books and usually left on the desk. Both Jean and I need access to them. But it was at least a week before I could take a look at Rupert's.'

'And what did you see?' The Dame's voice was eager, the reprimand forgotten.

'I saw that on the afternoon that Phoebe ran into Sheila in London, Rupert had scribbled across the page one word: Lordstanding.'

'But that means that he went there when Mrs Bassano was on her own. His visit must have been nothing to do with the Rubies.'

'Exactly. And why else would our bright young duke take himself off to Lordstanding?'

'There may be a perfectly simple explanation,' the Dame suggested; she knew well the dangers of leaping to conclusions.

'Indeed there may,' Tom agreed. 'But I have noticed that recently Rupert has taken to going off for hours at a time. He doesn't make a note in his diary any more and nobody knows where he is.'

'That sounds bad. But I'm reluctant to believe that Rupert could behave irresponsibly.' Even as she spoke, Dame Elizabeth found herself remembering the words of the old dowager – Rupert's grandmother – who had declared that all the Jordans men were weak when it came to attractive women. And Jamey, Rupert's father, had shown himself thoroughly irresponsible when he fell into the clutches of Bubbles Fiske. Was history to repeat itself? She glanced across the room: Diana was chatting away happily to her brother-in-law, and although she looked a little tired, that was only to be expected after the move and the preparations for Christmas: there seemed no sign that the new duchess was worried about her duke.

The Dame would have liked to explore further with her brother the fascinating topic of Rupert's dalliance, but they were now joined by Lady Alice.

'I've left my mob,' she said breezily, 'to come and talk to my friends.'

They all looked across to a group gathered closely

together, as if for safety, under one of the tall sash windows. Lady Alice's house party was a recognised social hazard in Mallamshire life: she was apt to fill her house with a motley collection – a minor television face, a young actor or two, a brace of models all leavened with the odd oil-rich Arab – and these she would take around with her, arriving hours late and unannounced at the homes of her friends, who had learned from the experience of having to cater for six or seven more mouths than expected to be very firm indeed with Lady Alice.

'I'm taking them all to Lordstanding tomorrow,' Alice went on.

'Then you won't be at the Manor of Braye?'

'No, I think Betty Bassano's party will be more our speed than the Mallabys'. Betty has the Fingelsteins staying, and I used to know Joe Fingelstein very well indeed at one time.'

There was a lubricious brightness in Lady Alice's fine, raddled eyes as she spoke, and the Dame smiled despite herself.

'Will you be at Lordstanding, Dame E.?'

'No. Mrs Bassano was kind enough to ask me – she seems to be spreading her net very wide – but I always go to Andrew and Angela on Boxing Day and I'm too old for two parties on the same day.'

Lady Alice drifted off, leaving the Dame with a faint sense of exasperation. It was, she supposed, in character for Alice to choose the smart newcomer's party rather than that of old friends; but recently Alice had shown signs of sense, of devotion to Mallamshire, and had kept her head in the recent row over Barnaby's Charity. It would be a pity if Alice found herself in Mrs Bassano's camp, for the time might come when the Dame would want to enlist her support to keep her nephew in order.

By the effulgent Christmas tree, Diana was listening to her brother-in-law as he told her about the meeting in

London he had attended as a newly appointed trustee. At the same time, like all hostesses, she was keeping a watchful eye on the wellbeing of her party, the circulation of drinks and the offering of canapés. When James, the footman, passed, bearing an entrée dish filled with cheese straws, she stayed him.

'James, isn't it time you fetched Molly's vol-au-vents?'

'I don't know, Your Grace,' he mumbled. 'These here are what Aggie Smiles gave me to serve.'

'Well, go and find Molly and tell her to bring out her pastries before everyone leaves.'

More hunchbacked than ever, James went muttering on his way and Diana turned to Colin with apology.

'I'm sorry, you were going to tell me about the rubies.'

'They came up at the board meeting. The trustees are beginning to be worried that Rupert has made no progress in retrieving any of the missing heirlooms from Sheila.'

'He's been to see her several times, I know,' she told him defensively, 'but Sheila is proving rather difficult to pin down.'

'Perhaps it's a mistake to leave it to Rupert,' Colin suggested. 'The board has a feeling he's dragging his feet.'

'Why should he do that? I'm sure he's pursuing Sheila as tactfully as he can.'

'Maybe. But you might tip him the wink that if he doesn't produce a result soon, the board will have recourse to lawyers.'

'Yes, I'll tell him.' Diana sighed. 'I've kept out of it, but he is finding it tiresome, and I know he wants to avoid the publicity involved in legal action.'

'He'll have to pull his finger out, in that case,' said Colin. He looked down at his sister-in-law's triangular face with its firm jaw-line. He was fond of Diana, and knew she was a good wife to his brother; he had heard too, from his mother, of her concern that Rupert had

been over to Lordstanding rather more often than
might seem necessary. It had to be admitted that Bessy
Bassano was undeniably attractive. He hoped that Diana
wasn't going to be hurt. To divert her, he now asked if
she was going to Lordstanding tomorrow.

'I don't know why everyone keeps asking me that,'
said Diana crossly. 'Rupert and I will be at the Manor of
Braye: we go to the Mallabys' every Boxing Day, and
after that, we'll be quietly at home with the boys. We
don't see nearly enough of them together.'

Boxing Day did not work out as Diana had hoped.
They were in the car on their way to the Manor of Braye
when Rupert broke his news.

'We needn't stay very long at the Mallabys', need we? I
mean, we'll just look in for a drink and then we can go
straight on to Lordstanding.'

Diana, who was driving, swerved, narrowly missing
one of the stone parapets on the three-arched stone
bridge that gave Rockport its name.

'What are you talking about, Rupert? We're not going
to Mrs Bassano's party.'

'Oh yes we are – I accepted ages ago.'

'But you can't have. You didn't even consult me.'

'Of course I did.' Rupert's tone was reasonable. 'We
talked about it when we were having lunch at Mother's
before Christmas.'

'But we didn't say we'd go, Rupert – and you haven't
mentioned it since. I'm just not dressed for that sort of
smart party.'

As she spoke, Diana found herself thinking that it was
most unlike Rupert to be so inconsiderate. Her jaw set
firmly: she wasn't going to be bulldozed into
acquiescence. With an effort, she suppressed the rare
anger she felt rising inside her.

'I just don't want to have to suffer being patronised by
Sheila, and watch her fluttering around you. And I
don't want to have to be polite to all Mrs Bassano's

American friends, shown off as the new duchess and quite a nice little thing really.'

'That's not fair.' Rupert was keeping his voice sweet and level. 'Lots of our friends will be there – it'll be fun.'

'Can't you get it into your head that I don't want to go?' Diana took a deep breath and controlled her voice. 'We planned to have a quiet Christmas in our new home, just us and the boys. Goodness knows, we spend little enough time with them as it is, and Christmas is meant for the children.'

'We spent all yesterday with them: aren't we entitled to a little fun ourselves?'

'Mrs Bassano's party is not my idea of fun. I'm not going, and that's all there is to it.'

'Very well,' Rupert hissed back, restraint gone, 'I shall go on my own.'

'But Rupert,' her voice rose in protest, 'you can't!'

'Why not?'

'Well, for one thing, we have only the one car. And I intend to go back home and have a quiet lunch with the boys.'

'No problem,' he replied, as if he had it all worked out, 'you can take a lift from Mother back from Braye and I'll take this car on to Lordstanding. After all,' he went on, returning to his air of reason, 'we're not Siamese twins: we don't have to do everything together.'

'Of course we're not – and that's why I feel that when we have a rare chance to be on our own, as a family, we ought to take it.'

Diana took her eyes off the road for a moment and glanced sideways at her husband. He was sitting rigid, staring straight ahead, his mouth shut like an iron bar across his face. It was clear he had nothing more to say. Although he was behaving like a self-willed little boy, Diana felt for a moment a pang of regret that she had been so definite in her refusal to go along with him. She would have liked to let him have his way; but she was determined not to give in.

In any case, it was too late for second thoughts. By now, they had reached Braye and were turning off the main road by the green down into the narrow lane that led to the Manor. With an effort, Diana pinned a bright social smile on to her face and prepared to make their entrance to the Mallabys' gathering appear amicable.

Rupert did not stay long. After a brief word with his host and another with his mother, a nod to Dame Elizabeth and a few courtesies to Angela, he downed his drink and was off. Diana made sure his mother overheard her tell him cheerfully to have a good time and not to hurry home.

Dame Elizabeth, who was standing next to Lorna Jordans, also heard this exchange, and she looked to see how Rupert's mother took it. The two women made a strange contrast: Lorna, tall and elegant in grey jersey wool, the Dame stalwart, four-square, with her pepper-and-salt hair swept back from her weatherbeaten face into a bun and her broad figure wrapped in a red quilted jacket decorated with strange, string-like frogging that she had picked up during her travels in the Balkans. Each was wondering if the other knew the significnce of Rupert's abrupt departure. They had come together as allies to fight a monstrous planning application for a vast development on the edge of the market town of Mallaby; subsequently, the Dame had proved a wise counsellor during Lorna's divorce.

They knew each other's thoughts. But the Dame gave an almost imperceptible shake of her head, and Lorna nodded agreement. That Rupert was indulging in an affair with Betty Bassano, though regrettable, was at the moment his own business. It would only be if and when it became known more generally that conference might be necessary and even then, much would depend on Diana's reaction. So they chatted instead about Rupert's research into the Carracci Aphrodite. Then, to the Dame's surprise, they were joined by Lady Alice.

'I thought you were going to Lordstanding today,' said the Dame accusingly.

'I was,' Lady Alice admitted, 'and I've sent my mob over there. But I'm quite glad to be shot of them for a bit – Christmas goes on for so long – and I decided after all to come to Braye. Old friends come first at this time of the year.'

Dame Elizabeth nodded approvingly – perhaps Alice's heart was in the right place after all – and after Lorna had drifted off to talk to Andrew Mallaby, she decided that the time was ripe to broach an idea that had taken root in her mind.

'You know Mrs Bassano well, don't you?'

'Fairly well,' said Alice. 'We've met at odd times in different parts of the world and we have friends in common. Why do you ask?'

'I'm beginning to think I'd like to get to know her a bit better. I only met her briefly, after the memorial service at Rockport, but it seems she's beginning to figure prominently in Mallamshire life.'

'No problem: I'll take you over to Lordstanding whenever you like.'

The Dame shook her head. 'I'd rather meet her somewhere else.'

She knew well that people behaved more revealingly when they were away from the security of their own home background.

'No problem again,' said Lady Alice. 'Betty plays a good hand of bridge. Why don't you lay on one of your evenings and I'll bring her along?'

'Excellent,' the Dame agreed. She was well used to Alice's skill in the arrangement of entertainment in the homes of her friends. 'Who shall we have as a fourth? We'd better make it a hen party and I don't know any other women players.'

'Why, Sheila, of course. She played well at one time, she says, although she gave it up when she married Jamey as he hated cards.'

'That's very neat – I've been thinking for some time that I ought to do something about that tiresome little woman.'

Seven

At Lordstanding, Betty Bassano was in her favourite room, the one the interior decorator had called the library. It was dominated by a fine bow window facing west and here Betty stood, looking out over the prospect. Beyond a broad plateau, the land dropped away to a valley where the river meandered through lush pasture, its banks lined with clumps of willow. Here, in the summer, cows would browse, as much part of the carefully composed landscape as the fine stands of beech that crowned the hill beyond. Now, in deep winter, all was mantled by a thin covering of snow; the wan sunlight of the January afternoon slanted across the invisible lawn, casting deep blue shadows under the trees, whose bare branches rose, still and black, against a steely sky. It was not, Betty conceded, as spectacular as an American winter; but in its understated way it was an exhilarating sight. And it was England. For, after nearly twenty years in the United States, Betty was glad that she had come home.

She was still amazed by the turn of the wheel that had brought her to Mallamshire and to Lordstanding. Even all those years ago, when the fourteen-year-old Betty Box, in shabby hard hat and mud-spattered jeans, had brought her borrowed pony to a halt in the river valley to stare up at the blank windows of the handsome stone house, she had never dreamed that one day she would be staring down at the view from one of those windows, mistress of that house – and a great deal more besides.

Betty glanced down at the carriage clock on her desk. She was waiting the return of Sheila Jordans, who had taken herself off to London on the excuse of some shopping. Sheila was being most tactful and discreet: though nothing was said, she managed to learn when Rupert was expected at Lordstanding and generally contrived her absence. And yesterday evening, quietly alone with Rupert, had been as good as ever – thanks to Sheila's sensibility. And there was more that she owed to her house-guest. It had been good luck that, after the memorial service for Jamey, Betty had met so many delightful Mallamshire folk; but she was no fool and she realised that the presence of a duchess at Lordstanding could only enhance her own social reputation.

The Boxing Day party had been a triumphant success. Betty was good at throwing parties, being generous and hospitable and well able to afford both. The American visitors had mixed well with her new Mallamshire friends, each forming a good opinion of the other, and she knew that word would soon spread in Palm Beach, Jackson Hole and other places where such things mattered that Betty Bassano had made a hit in her new home. True, Diana Jordans' absence had been a little conspicuous, despite Rupert's assurances to all that his wife always placed her duty before enjoyment and – though sorry to miss the junket – felt she had to spend the time with their children.

And it had been good to have Rupert there. Of course, with so many watchful eyes upon them, they could do no more than exchange the occasional half-smile across the chattering room; but it had given her a glow of content to watch him relaxing happily with her friends and his, away from his dutiful and – Betty thought – rather mousy little wife.

From the hall, Betty could now hear the sounds that told her Sheila was back. Pedro's excited voice was raised in greeting as he assmbled Sheila's suitcases. Then the telephone rang: Betty moved to the receiver but before she reached it a ping told her that Sheila had answered it in the hall and was now having a merry conversation with the caller. Betty frowned: Sheila made a habit of answering all calls and seemed to assume they were all for her, or made them so. It was beginning to irritate. So when Sheila came into the library at last, and after an effusive greeting, Betty asked shortly who had been on the phone.

'It was old Bessie de Blete,' said Sheila chirpily, 'she's some sort of cousin to my first husband, and we had a lot of news to exchange.'

'Is that the old trout who dresses like a Bulgarian peasant? I think I met her at Rockport.'

'That's the one: and she's asked us over for dinner and bridge next week. Alice will be there to make up the four.'

'Do we have to go?' Betty drawled. A female foursome was not her idea of an exciting evening.

'Oh yes. You mustn't be taken in by her appearance: Dame Elizabeth has friends high and low throughout the county. Everyone takes her advice, everyone listens to what she has to say, and she could be a very useful ally – if the time comes, my dear, when you need allies.'

Sheila accompanied this last remark with a significant look. She was well aware of the progress of her hostess's involvement with her stepson Rupert: it suited her book very well to have the new duke a constant visitor at Lordstanding, and it would suit her even better should Betty ever become his second duchess: Betty was attractive and very rich and much more suitable, in Sheila's opinion, than Diana, who was after all only the daughter of a publican.

But Betty did not respond to her hint, so she began to talk of her stay in London, of whom she had seen and where she had dined.

'Actually,' she continued, 'I'm thinking of buying a flat in town. Wherever I live – and I haven't made up my mind yet – it seem sensible to take a place in London. It would be a base for Josh, and he needs that, poor darling.'

Sheila's son, the wayward baronet Sir Joshua Fiske, must now be touching forty, Betty thought, and no longer in need of his mother's apron strings. He had been a frequent visitor to Lordstanding, treating the house like his home and coming and going without warning. Betty had made him welcome for his mother's sake; but she considered his brand of dissolute charm was wearing a bit thin, and he clearly regarded his mother as a financial crutch. Of her other son, who was an accountant in Manchester with a wife and two daughters, Sheila seldom spoke. An apartment in London was a new idea, and Betty found herself wondering where the money was to come from: she had a fairly shrewd idea of how much Jamey had left to his widow, and flats in London were mighty expensive these days.

It was not the time to ask about this, however, for the white-coated manservant had now entered, with the mail for Sheila that had arrived that morning. She thanked him and added,

'Could we have some tea, please, Pedro? I'm dying for a cup after my journey.'

She began to scrutinise her envelopes and Betty experienced another twinge of irritation. It was a bit much that Sheila ordered the servants around as if they were her own, without a word to her hostess. She was for ever asking Maria to do some ironing and Pedro to fetch and carry. Still, Betty reminded herself, she had insisted that Sheila treat Lordstanding as her own home, so she could hardly complain when her guest did exactly that.

Sheila was now reading one of her letters, spectacles

on her nose and a pinched frown about her eyebrows.

'Oh Lord,' she said, suddenly subdued, 'I've been summoned into the presence.'

'My dear, what on earth do you mean?'

Sheila handed over the letter. It was on thick, cream-laid paper with, discreetly embossed in black, the legend 'Jordans Estate Office, Somersham Place, London W.' The superscription was in full, to 'Her Grace Sheila, Duchess of Jordans' and it opened with a fine flourish of bold black handwriting 'Dear Madam'.

Betty read on.

'I have been advised by my fellow trustee Lord Colin Delaney-Grey that you are continuing to stay with friends in Mallamshire. Some months have now elapsed since the demise of your late husband, and I judge it may now be useful for us to confer together. The trustees are anxious to explain to you the various provisions they have it in their power to make for the widow of his late Grace, and thus such a meeting may also prove to your advantage.

'You will be welcome here at any time to suit your convenience and I myself look forward to the privilege of receiving you.

'With my personal condolences and good wishes,

'I remain, dear Madam,

    'Yours faithfully,

    'A.C. Dunhill.'

Betty read it though again, then folded it and handed it back to Sheila.

'What a grim little note,' she remarked. 'And who exactly is Mr A.C. Dunhill?'

'He's the senior trustee,' Sheila explained. 'From what

Jamey told me, I gather he's the power behind the scenes. He runs the whole network that looks after the family money and what he says goes. I know Jamey had a dreadful time from him when he was divorcing Lorna. I've never met him and I don't want to.'

'I don't think you can refuse him,' said Betty. 'Rupert has told me something about the way his family runs their finances and it sounds as if you'd be unwise to offend this Mr Dunhill.'

'You may be right. Jamey said he was a wily old thing; but there are other trustees – Colin for one, and he's always been very friendly towards me.'

Betty gave Sheila a careful look. Perhaps the time had come to honour the promise she had given Rupert that when it seemed apt, she would have a word about the missing heirlooms.

'Has it occurred to you that, reading between the lines of that letter, there may be more involved than what Mr Dunhill calls provision for the widow?'

'What do you mean?' Sheila snapped.

'I mean, my dear, the Rockport rubies, among other things. Rupert has talked to me about them, and I know he's very anxious to conclude his research into that picture he's discovered.'

'Rupert has talked to me about them too, though he's dropped the subject in the past month. But I think all that business about his research is just a blind. He wants me to hand over all the lovely things my darling Jamey gave me, and that I have no intention of doing.'

'But Sheila, if they are not your property, then you must return them.'

'Why should I?' Sheila's delicately plucked eyebrows arched and her bright little eyes were suddenly hard, defensive.

'In the first place, because perhaps they weren't Jamey's to give to you. And think, if you do hand them back gracefully, you'll build up a useful credit of goodwill with the trustees: whereas, if you hang on to them, you'll have a tough fight on your hands.'

'I'm not afraid of a fight – not that it will come to that.' Sheila got up and moved over to sit beside Betty on the sofa. 'Look, you've been a good friend to me, and I appreciate that you must speak your mind. But you yourself know only too well what it's like for a woman on her own. The men think they hold all the cards, that all we have to do is to be grateful for the few crumbs they're gracious enough to throw in our direction.'

'But surely you're not dependent on the trustees?'

'Not entirely,' Sheila concluded, 'Jamey left me a bit. But it's not enough for the standard of living I'm entitled to. And my ace of trumps is the jewellery. If I have possession of what they want back – and, mind you, I haven't admitted that I do – then what they call the heirlooms and I call Jamey's presents to me can sit in my bank vault on the other side of the Atlantic until the trustees come up to scratch.'

'And what do you consider scratch?' Betty was dubious about the morality of her friend's stand but she admired her guts.

'A suitable income, of course: a decent flat in London and perhaps a place in the country. The family have an empty house not far from here which might do very well.'

'I see.' Betty was impressed, and she fell silent as she began to sort out her loyalties. Rupert, thank goodness, was no longer involved in the battle to come: his place had been taken by these faceless trustees. And she had fulfilled her promise to him: Sheila knew exactly what she wanted and was not to be talked out of her high ground. She reminded herself of Sheila's kindness and affection during her own troubled times: now was not the time to quibble about ethics – she must declare herself for Sheila.

'I wish you all the luck in the world,' she said. 'But if

you ask me, I think you ought to set about finding yourself a tough lawyer of your own. You don't want to go into a meeting with the trustees without a sound profeesional beside you.'

'Good idea, darling,' said Sheila, 'do you know of one?'

The two women looked blankly at each other. Betty was equipped with a battery of attorneys in the United States, and Sheila had the services of a skilled firm in the Bahamas: but neither of them knew of a sound, hard-headed English solicitor.

'I know,' said Betty at last – and it was a measure of her understanding of her new home territory that she made the suggestion – 'I know, next week, we can ask Dame Elizabeth.'

Eight

On the day appointed for Dame Elizabeth's bridge party, a high wind rose, driving squalls of rain across the land. In a few hours, the snow had dispersed into gutters and gulleys. The Dame, who had been out to the village shop for a last-minute purchase of some baking apples and fresh cream, scurried back across the sodden grass of the village green. Wicket Cottage – her home since her retirement from the Civil Service and from London – greeted her cheerfully. Under the stone roof, sleek as a seal's back under the onslaught of the storm, its neat casement windows glowing from the lamps lit within, beamed a welcome, and as she closed her garden gate and found shelter under the porch, she felt a surge of love for her warm, bright house.

The Dame was well versed in preparing for her evening. Over the years, she had enjoyed many such, with a group of friends who between them exercised such an influence behind the scenes in the life of the county that they had become known as Dame Elizabeth's junta; but of late, the junta had fallen apart, due to absence or ill-health of some of its members, and only Lady Alice remained, so, as she went about laying the table and looking out bridge scorers and pencils, she found she was much looking forward to the occasion, both for the prospect of some challenging cards and for the chance to take a good look at the unknown newcomer who had, it seemed, entangled herself with

Rupert Jordans.

The dinner would be good. A few days ago, the Dame had found at her back door a brace of pheasants hanging in their gaudy plumage. She had known at once that they were a thank-offering from old Gabriel Platt, the village's retired roadman and still-practising poacher. Old Gabriel had run into some trouble over his pension rights and Dame Elizabeth had joined battle in his behalf: the birds were his way of expressing his gratitude. And luckily, for the Dame was not well versed in practical country matters and had no skill in the messy business of plucking, Becky Grimble at the shop was a dab hand at dressing birds for the table and always happy to oblige.

With the pheasants placed in a casserole under a rich sauce to simmer in the oven, with the wine drawn, the curtains closed and the fire lit, Dame Elizabeth took herself up to bath and change. Then came the pleasant, anticipatory hour when, with all ready for her guests, she could sit back with a whisky and wonder which would be the first to arrive. Her sitting-room gave her pleasure: it had been formed by knocking two small parlours together, and with its white painted beams and one wall lined with books, spoke very much of its owner's personality – warm, friendly, with a wide-ranging intelligence and an active curiosity. There was a broad-beamed wing-chair with needlework cushions next to the fire: beside this stood a round table laden with a good lamp and a stack of journals, and below it was a shabby stool, the property of the Dame's cat, a fine blue-pointed Siamese.

The cat now stretched itself luxuriously and the Dame decided she might as well let it out into the garden before her guests arrived. The rain had stopped, but the gale was still blustering over the downs, sending tattered shreds of cloud to scud across the harried moon. As she stood in her porch, enjoying the wind in her face, she saw two pairs of headlights turn off the main road and make their way down the lane. Her party had arrived, and she hurried them into the warmth.

They stood together in the middle of the room as Dame Elizabeth fetched drinks. Betty Bassano was looking around, taking in as discreetly as she could the details of the room, when her attention was caught by a small painting of a Madonna and Child in a gilded gesso frame that hung, discreetly lit, above the Dame's desk. It was of such quality, and by so far the finest thing in the room, that she exclaimed how lovely it was.

'Ah,' said the Dame with a smile, handing her a vodka and tonic, 'you've spotted my most treasured possession. I've always nourished a passion for Italian primitives,' she explained, 'ever since as a girl I spent a few months in Tuscany. But they are far beyond what I could afford: that was a lovely present from Angela and Andrew Mallaby when they came back from their honeymoon in Florence.'

The approving look in the Dame's eye suggested that Mrs Bassanno had, by her enthusiasm for the painting, scored a good point in her favour.

There was now some discussion as to how they should play. Sheila Jordans suggested that Lordstanding should play as a team, but Dame Elizabeth wouldn't have that. She knew that she could learn a lot from a player's behaviour at the card table, both as a partner and adversary, so she insisted they should cut for every rubber. Thus, the Dame drew Sheila, and Betty and Alice would play together.

As they settled, Sheila shuffling with a croupier's expertise, the four women presented a strange contrast. Dame Elizabeth was robed in a tent-like kaftan of peacock blue with gold-threaded hems and cuffs, a majestic if eccentric garment, and Lady Alice wore a suede waistcoat over a tan dress with a yellow scarf tied loosely at the neck, perfectly suitable garb for the occasion. Betty Bassano was, again, acceptable in a scarlet trouser-suit; while Sheila Jordans had chosen a lavender coat and skirt with, slung over her thin shoulders, an angora stole. She had been anxious, she had said to Betty on the way over, about the prospect of draughts in the Dame's little cottage: not that she need have worried; for Dame Elizabeth's standard of personal comfort was high and her house was always warm, thanks to the vast boiler she had installed before moving in, which the awestruck builder had said would drive a train to London and back.

The first rubber was uneventful, the players taking each other's measure. Sheila Jordans proved to be a greedy partner, avid to play every hand, pursing her lips with annoyance when she lost a trick. Lady Alice was dashing and impetuous, and since Betty Bassano proved to be an adventurous bidder, they made a spirited partnership, sometimes scoring well and sometimes going down spectacularly. When they drew the line, the score was even, and the Dame now suggested they adjourn for dinner.

It was while they were enjoying the pheasant casserole that Sheila Jordans decided to put her question.

'Dear coz,' she cooed, 'this stew is quite delicious, I do adore simple peasant food. But may I ask your advice? I know you have Mallamshire at your fingertips.'

Dame Elizabeth assented amiably enough; but inwardly she winced. She wished the fluffy little woman wouldn't always make so much of a kinship that was so remote as to be forgotten.

'The fact is,' Sheila went on, 'I am on the look-out for a bright lawyer here in England and I thought you might be able to recommend one to me.'

Her tone was that of a woman making a casual enquiry for a chiropodist; but while the Dame was thinking about a suitable name, Lady Alice leapt in.

'If you want a chap here in Mallamshire,' she said, 'there's no one better than Mr Dean in Shipston. We use him at Barnaby's Charity and I can tell you there are no flies on him when it comes to the law.'

'Mr Dean is indeed an excellent solicitor,' Dame Elizabeth agreed, 'but I fancy he would find himself unable to accept Sheila as a client.'

'Why not?' asked Sheila sharply. 'If he's the best man, he's the man for me.'

'It's not as simple as that. It might be embarrassing for Mr Dean, even if there was no conflict of interest. You see, Mr Dean already acts for Lorna.'

'Damn, I'd forgotten that. Never mind, I'm sure Dame E. can think of somebody else.' Lady Alice took a swig of her wine.

'I'll try and make some suggestions, but first I need to know the kind of man you need and what sort of advice you want.'

Sheila was silent. She seemed quite put out that her predecessor Lorna had got in first with the estimable Mr Dean.

'After all,' the Dame pursued, 'you have all the resources of the Rockport trustees at your disposal. I don't quite see why you want a man of your own.'

'Sheila is thinking of taking a house in Mallamshire,' Betty put into the silence, 'so she'll need a lawyer for that.'

'Well, if it's just a matter of conveyancing, you won't need a high-powered firm.' The Dame looked closely at Sheila: there was more to this than the purchase of property.

'We're all women on our own,' Sheila said at last, 'and we all know what that's like. I'm only just getting used to the fact that my darling Jamey isn't here to take care of all the beastly business; and although the trustees are very efficient, I just feel I want to have someone of my own to advise me professionally.'

'So you're squaring up for a fight with the trustees, are you, Sheila?' Alice sounded amused. 'I've had to live with them all my life, and I've never won a battle with them yet.'

'I know.' Sheila smiled at her sister-in-law. 'Jamey told me he had a horrid time with old Mr Dunhill at the time of his divorce. That's why I need a lawyer of my own, to stand up to him.'

'Why?' The Dame's single word was accompanied by a stern glare.

'Why?' Sheila repeated. 'Because I have to make sure that my own interests are protected, that's why.'

'And I take it that you fear your view of your interests may not coincide with that of the trustees.'

'Something like that, yes.' Sheila was beginning to feel a little uncomfortable under the Dame's cross-examination: her fingers twitched at her stole. The dame noticed that the emerald ring she had spotted on the little duchess's finger after the memorial service was not now being displayed; to give herself a little time before the next question, she rose to clear away the plates and fetch the sizzling baked apples from the oven.

'I think,' said the Dame as she passed the cream, 'that Sheila would be best advised to go to one of the better London firms for legal advice. They'll be sure to have someone expert in dealing with family trusts, and from what you say that's what you need.'

Behind the thought was the hope that Sheila might stay well away from Mallamshire, once she left the shelter of Mrs Bassano's house; but this hope was dashed by what the little duchess had to say next.

'I'm planning to live down here again, you know,' she said. 'Not all the time, but I think it is where I belong.'

'Oh really?' Lady Alice was bored, and itching to get back to the cards. 'Have you anywhere in mind?'

'Between ourselves, I have. But I can't tell you until it's settled. It will be up to Rupert, bless him.'

This was the first time in the evening that Rupert's name had come up: none of them wanted to dwell on it, and the Dame quickly proposed that they return to the table to have their coffee there.

This time, Dame Elizabeth cut with Betty Bassano, which suited her very well. After a few hands, their partnership developed into a solid understanding: they were making the most of every hand and their score mounted steadily. They finished with a triumph: a grand slam in spades which Sheila rashly and petulantly doubled. Lady Alice took her sister-in-law's bid with a good-natured shrug: but Betty had something to say.

'Thank you, dear Sheila!' she crowed. 'Back in Jackson Hole, we'd call that the sucker's double. You've told me all I need to know to make my slam.'

And so it proved. By the time the scores were totted up, the Dame's partnership showed a healthy profit. The Dame was in high good spirits and Betty glowed with success, for a doubled grand slam doesn't come often. Lady Alice was congratulatory, for she had a cavalier attitude to cards and provided they were interesting, never minded losing. Sheila, however, was sulky, and muttered that she'd settle up with Betty later, when they got home.

'Oh no you don't,' said Betty firmly. 'The rule is that you pay to your right. You fork out to Dame Elizabeth.'

Reluctantly, Sheila fumbled in her purse and brought out a mass of small coins, which she pushed towards her hostess. Lady Alice already had her losses at hand and passed them to Betty, and the party from Lordstanding began to collect their scarves and bags and to take their leave. Betty Bassano was warm in her thanks to the Dame and urged that they should have another such evening at her house.

'We must give Sheila and Alice their chance of revenge,' she said, with a teasing look at the duchess.

The Dame went to the door to bid them good night,

then returned to wave Lady Alice back into her seat.

'Sheila doesn't much like losing, does she?' she remarked. 'I hope she doesn't go ahead with her plan to settle here in Mallamshire. To have three duchesses of Jordans all living within ten miles of each other would be very untidy.'

Untidiness in human affairs was a condition the Dame deplored.

'And if the total rose to four, it would be impossible,' said Lady Alice.

'Good heavens, Alice, you don't think the affair has gone that far, do you?' The Dame was horrified. 'Rupert may be behaving irresponsibly, but I can't believe he could be contemplating divorce and a second marriage.'

'Not yet, maybe.' Lady Alice shrugged. 'But in my experience, things have a habit of developing that way. Remember Jamey and Sheila? And Betty is charming and attractive, not to mention quite spectacularly rich.'

'H'm, you make her sound quite a catch – even for a duke. But my loyalty is to Diana. She's made a success of her marriage so far, and I'd hate to see it wrecked.'

'Oh, don't mistake me, I'm very fond of Diana, and she's been a good wife to Rupert. She'll make an excellent duchess too – but then, so would Betty, given the chance.'

'That is what worries me so much. If Betty were just a mistress on the side, someone of no particular consequence, then she wouldn't matter much. But she's not: she's a delightful young woman, and I really like her. That, my dear Alice, is why she is such a threat.'

Nine

In the Dutch parlour at Rockport, Diana Jordans was surprised to find herself feeling lonely. Rupert had taken himself off for his trip to Amsterdam to pursue his research into the rubies: it so happened that the date coincided with an engagement Diana was reluctant to break – the opening of a new museum in Somersham which she had promised to peform way back in the autumn – so she had been unable to go with him. The boys were back at school and Molly Platt was busy up in the nurseries, two storeys above; but the vast house still murmured with activity.

In the offices in the west wing, Tom de Blete and Jean Wright were both at work, attending to the administration of the estate and preparing their plans for the next tourist season. In the great saloon, two cleaning women were busy polishing tbe black-and-white marble floor; and there always, even in the depths of winter, seemed to be a bustle in the cobbled yard beyond the old kitchens: the woodman delivering logs, the head game-keeper to inquire about ordering more pheasant poults for the next shooting-season, the maintenance man tinkering with the clock that reared above the arch that led to the stables.

From time to time, she heard another sound, and one that puzzled her. It came to her intermittently, usually when she was enjoying her breakfast tray, although once it seemed even louder when, on a crisp and frosty morning, she had taken the boys out for a breath of air in the sparkling sunlight. It was a babble of voices broken occasionally by laughter, and sounded more like a cocktail party than anything else, although the voices were rougher than usual for such an assembly. Whatever it was, it added to her sense of isolation, of being cut off from the life of the house. When at last, she asked Rupert if he knew what was going on, he had merely shrugged and said it was probably the morning meeting of the estate workers, when they gathered to receive their orders for the day. This explanation Diana accepted, though with a doubt that such audible merriment was likely on a cold, dark winter's morning.

In the month since they had moved into Rockport Place, the Dutch parlour had become very much Diana's own. The seventeenth-century seascapes and flower paintings glowed on the green-painted walls, and there was a friendly disorder of books, magazines and children's toys on the wide stool in front of the fireplace: pots of hyacinths and azaleas stood on the sofa table, and on Diana's desk, a pretty Regency escritoire unearthed from a spare room, were photographs of Rupert and the boys. Here Diana settled herself. Before he left for the Netherlands, Rupert had suggested it was time they threw a full dinner party: with a blank morning before her, until she joined the boys for a quick lunch at Molly's kitchen table, she decided to make a list and compose the invitations and the menu.

The list itself was no problem. There were obligations to fulfil, people who would expect to be asked: the Lord Lieutenant, for instance, and the High Sheriff, who had obliged by their appearance at her father-in-law's memorial service: then there was the pleasant young judge from the Crown Court in Madderston whom Diana had met at a function and liked for his jollity. Add in a few friends, like the Mallabys and the

Lucktons, and it looked like being at least twenty people. That meant the state dining-room: and therefore she would have to conscript the help of the old butler and the footman.

She glanced at the bell, but decided against ringing. It often took over five minutes for Dobson to appear, after shrugging himself into his black coat and arming himself with a salver. Better by far to go and beard him in his den. After all, she told herself defiantly, this was her house, and she could do as she chose. So, after patting her dark hair into place and straightening her pearls, she set off through the baize door and down the echoing corridor that led to the old kitchen quarters. She was about to open the door to the butler's pantry when she heard from the old kitchen a loud hubbub of voices followed by a raucous laugh. So this was the source of the noise that had puzzled her. Curiosity conquered the butterflies in her stomach: Diana took a deep breath and marched in.

At first, she could not take in the sight before her. The long table was crowded, with six or seven people each side. The table itself was laden: plates piled high with sausages, eggs, bacon, fried bread, racks of toast and pots of home-made marmalade, steaming teapots and jugs of milk; on the dresser was a half-carved succulent pink ham and the tattered carcase of a roasted pheasant. Slowly the chatter died away as the startled faces turned to stare at the door. At the head of the table Dobson himself, in shirt-sleeves and braces, was frozen in the act of conveying a sausage to his mouth.

Slowly he set down his fork with a clatter and rose, dabbing at his lips with a napkin. Then, his eyebrows beetling censure, he spoke.

'Good-morning, Your Grace,' he said, 'I fear you have taken me by surprise. Is there anything amiss?'

'Yes, Dobson,' she snapped. 'I want to see you. In my sitting-room. In ten minutes. That will give you time to finish your breakfast.'

Her jaw-line very determined and her eyes hard, she turned and left the disconcerted party.

Back at her desk, Diana tried to calm her anger. That Dobson and his cronies were living it up, at the expense of her household budget, enraged her. She knew quite well that for someone born to Rockport Place, there would have been nothing surprising in the old servants doing themselves well on the quiet. But Diana was not born to the purple, she was the daughter of a successful publican and she could make a shrewd guess at the cost of entertaining what looked like half the village population to a morning spread. And she resented being thought a fool.

To prepare her ground for the advent of the butler, she began to make a note of the people around the table whom she had recognised. Diana was good at names, and since coming to Rockport she had been at some trouble to get to know the staff, outside and inside, who served the engines that powered the great house. Dobson and Mrs Smiles, as host and hostess, had sat at either end of the table, and James had been hovering around the ham. Fair enough, but what had Mr Dunt, the gamekeeper, the head gardener Mr Boggis and the odd-job man who cleaned the cars and sometimes acted as chauffeur been doing there, let alone Aggie Smiles' nephew Jock who was a bit wanting and swept the car parks, old Mrs Prendergast who was the widow of the old duke's groom and lived in one of the lodges, the postman and the village policeman, what right had all this company to the hospitality of her house? Even the two cleaning women, who should have been on their knees in the great saloon, had been spotted sitting back with a cup of tea and a fat slice of fruit cake.

'You wished to see me, Your Grace?' Dobson was in the room.

'Yes, Dobson.' From her chair at the desk, Diana paused deliberately to stare up at the old man's

impassive face. 'What on earth was going on just now?
No, don't tell me' – she waved a hand at him – 'I can
guess. It's got to stop, Dobson. No more breakfast
parties. Is that understood?'

'But, Your Grace, it's an ancient custom. For years it
has been the practice that Mrs Smiles keeps open house,
and His late Grace never …'

'No, Dobson. Whatever may have gone on during the
time of my husband's grandfather, my mind is made up.
Of course, you and Mrs Smiles and James are resident
here, and fully entitled to your board. I just don't want
you entertaining most of Mallamshire at my expense.'

Dobson's white eyebrows were signalling furious
disapproval, but Diana found, quite suddenly, that they
had lost their power to daunt her. In the end it was the
butler's eyes that dropped; murmuring 'Very good,
Your Grace', he turned to leave.

'One moment, Dobson,' she called after him, 'I have
something else to tell you. I'm planning a big dinner
party in February: we'll be using the state dining-room.
I thought I'd give you plenty of warning: I want to use
the Paul Storr silver gilt, and I'll need both you and
James to serve, for I'm expecting at least twenty people.
And His Grace would like you to attend to the wine.'

Rupert hadn't said anything of the kind, but after her
victory, Diana wanted to restore the old man's *amour
propre*.

'Very good, Your Grace,' he repeated, but in a much
less lugubrious tone. 'If I am to see to the wines, I shall
need to have notice of the proposed menu. For such an
occasion in the days of His late Grace, Mrs Smiles always
served turtle soup, fillet of sole in a white sauce, roast
saddle of mutton, chocolate mousse and angels on
horseback. There will be a requirement for additional
hands in the kitchens, of course, but I'm sure Your
Grace …'

'No, Dobson,' Diana interrupted very firmly indeed.

'If Mrs Smiles is capable of producing a breakfast on the scale I saw this morning, then I'm sure she'd have no difficulty in cooking a simple dinner for my guests. But the need won't arise: Molly Platt will be in charge of the catering and the dinner will be served from her kitchen. We will start with a smoked salmon confection she does beautifully, then have some venison marinated in red wine, then a pudding and cheese.'

'Very well, Your Grace. I will inspect the cellars and make some suggestions as to the appropriate wines to His Grace when he returns. But if I might mention it, I must say that Mrs Smiles will be mortified at the service of a dinner here in which she has no part. She is, if I may say so, proud of her gooseberry pies and famous for them. Perhaps ...?'

'All right, Dobson,' Diana said. Molly wasn't best at puddings, and the old kitchens might as well do something to earn their keep. Besides, if Dobson had his way, they'd be debating the matter all morning, and she had other things to do. 'We'll have the pies. And that will be all,' she told him with finality.

Dobson processed back through the baize door and down to Aggie Smiles's kitchen, where she, James and the odd-job-man looked expectantly at thim.

'Put Her young Grace in her place, have you, Mr Dobson?' she asked.

'No, Mrs Smiles. Her Grace knows her place as I know mine. Hers is to give orders to the likes of us, and ours is to carry 'em out. So there'll be no more breakfasts – not for the likes of you.' He turned to scowl fiercely at the odd-job man. 'Haven't you any work to do?'

The man scuttled away, muttering to himself, 'Mean I call it, mean, after all these years.'

Dobson turned to Mrs Smiles. 'Now then, Aggie, Her Grace is planning a slap-up dinner, just like the old days: and she has asked specially if you might oblige with your gooseberry pie.'

'Well now, Mr Dobson, I might at that. I've got a fair number of bottles I put up last summer, and it'd be a pleasure to be getting my hands on some pastry again. Heard of my pies, has she upstairs?'

'Oh yes. She says you're famous for them.'

'Imagine that, Mr Dobson.' Aggie was deeply gratified.

At her desk in the Dutch parlour, Diana was quite unaware of the new-found favour her firmness – and Dobson's diplomacy – had earned her below stairs. She was engaged on the pleasant task of writing out her invitations, for which she was using some old writing paper found in a box in the business-room. The paper was thick and white, embossed at the head with the simple legend 'Rockport Place, Mallamshire' in a heavy Gothic face. Her pen enjoyed the work as she bent to inscribe the formula. '*Dear Mrs Makepeace, My husband and I will be delighted if you and the General …*'

With the job done, she realised that, with her brother-in-law Colin certain to be present, she was short of one woman. Her address book seemed a little light on unattached ladies of Colin's age: then she remembered Mrs Bassano. Rupert had been on at her to invite the newcomer to Rockport before Christmas, she remembered: now was the perfect opportunity. Not having the address, she decided to go through to the office and ask Jean. So she gathered up her envelopes and left the Dutch parlour, passing the two cleaning ladies now ostentatiously back at work with mop and duster in the great saloon.

In the office, Jean looked up with a bright smile from her typewriter.

'You might post these for me,' said Diana, placing her stack of envelopes on the table. 'I'm going to give a big dinner party next month for all the nobs, so you'd better list the names in the diary.'

'Good for you,' said Jean, 'It's about time the big house did a bit of entertaining for the county.'

'And do you have the telephone number for Lordstanding? I want to ask Mrs Bassano: she seems to have made quite a hit socially, and I feel it's time we had her to Rockport.'

Jean looked away, suddenly flustered; she fumbled in her address book before muttering that she didn't seem to have the number to hand.

'Perhaps it would be better to send her a written invitation like the others,' she added. 'I'll do the letter for you now if you want.'

'Thanks, Jean, but I think I'd better telephone. I want to explain why I can't ask Sheila, and that's easier done by word of mouth. I'll go and look in Rupert's book: he's rung her house quite a bit, I know, over those wretched rubies and he's bound to have the number.'

Diana went off to the business-room, and soon returned with a slip of paper.

'By the way, Jean,' she said, 'did you know about Aggie Smiles's breakfast parties in the old kitchen?'

'Sort of,' Jean admitted. 'I've known something was going on since I came here, but everyone seemed to close their eyes. I did warn you back in November that the bills for provisions were high.'

'So you did. Well, I've told Dobson it's got to stop. There must have been sixteen people around the table this morning when I chanced to look in. Sometimes I think I'm the last person in this house to hear what's going on.'

Hearing the young duchess's footsteps retreating up the stone corridor, Jean found herself reflecting that she had spoken truer than she knew; and she just hoped that when Diana got through to Lordstanding, Betty Bassano would have her wits about her.

In the Dutch parlour, Diana reached for her instrument and dialled the number. It was answered at once, in a thick foreign accent.

'May I speak to Mrs Bassano please?' Diana made her

voice very clear.

'So sorry, Señora Bassano is away. No here.'

'Away?' Diana wondered if the newcomer had by a whim returned to America. 'When will she be back?'

'Señora is in Holland. Amsterdam, she say. Back on Tuesday.'

Amsterdam! It was as if the word was shrieked at her. She was silent for so long that the voice at the other end began to quack, ''Allo? 'Allo?'

Without replying, she replaced the receiver, got up and went to stare out of the tall sash window. It was a bleak, scowling winter's day: scudding rain rattled the panes and suddenly Diana felt very very cold.

All at once, her thoughts fell into place. That Rupert was with Betty Bassano in Amsterdam was obvious: and that he must have been carrying on with her for some time. All the evasions and inconsistencies, all Rupert's unexplained absences and all his late returns home now made sense. She even remembered the odd incident that Tom de Blete had reported several months ago, when his wife had been cut dead by Sheila Jordans in Harrod's. Obviously Sheila had not wanted to be seen in London when she was Rupert's excuse for a visit to Lordstanding.

Sheila must be in the know – and it would be to her advantage to encourage the affair. It was plain, too, from her behaviour that Jean was aware of something going on, something she was doing her best to keep from Diana: probably the whole household was agog about it, even the old servants below stairs – for servants always knew. Even Rupert's mother? Probably. Diana was beginning to recall odd, assessing looks from her friends and acquaintances: and into her mind there came the old saying that the wife is always the last to know.

Maybe: but, Diana added fiercely to herself, when the wife does know, she knows for certain.

As she wondered what action she should take, how best to contain the blaze that had broken out uncontrolled in the hearth of her marriage, she felt utterly alone. Despite a wide circle of warm friendships, she could think of no one in whom she might confide, from whom she could seek comfort and advice. For Rupert was her friend and her confidant, as well as her husband, her beloved lover and the father of their children – and she could hardly seek his advice. For it was Rupert who had deceived her, betrayed her, lied to her.

As these savage words ripped through her mind, she warned herself against being melodramatic, of over-reacting. For, since she first married into the Delaney-Greys, she had realised that, like most upper-class families, they possessed a casual, insouciant attitude to marital infidelity. Even when Rupert's father had started to carry on with Sheila, no one had minded very much – until he started to entertain thoughts of making her his Duchess. But for Diana, herself by birth and upbringing staunchly middle class, the marriage vows were serious. They served as a firm foundation in the intricate task of building a successful partnership for life: and to flout them rocked the edifice as in an earthquake.

She began to realise that Betty Bassano only represented a threat to her marriage if Diana made her so: if she was to bring the whole affair into the open, have a blazing row, admit her feelings of betrayal, then she might lose everything. But if she carried on as if still in blissful ignorance, told no one and admitted nothing, then all might not be lost. For to lose Rupert was a thought she could not, would not contemplate: he was hers and she loved him with an absoluteness that would be her strength in the days to come.

The decision made, she took a deep breath and felt better. There had as yet been no tears, only anger: and that must be damped down. Soon, the boys would be back from school, and she would have to face their sharp young eyes over the kitchen table – she had better go upstairs and effect some running repairs on her make-up. But before that, there was a job still to be done.

If the order of the day was to be, in the words of the old catch phrase from the Hitler War, Business as Usual, then the dinner party must go ahead. And Betty Bassano would be present. It would show the company that Diana's flag was still flying proudly, it might well disconcert Betty, and it might prove interesting to watch the two of them together under her eye. So she returned to her desk, took out another sheet of paper and began to write.

'Dear Mrs Bassano, My husband and I will be delighted if you will come to dine with us ...'

Ten

When Rupert telephoned from Amsterdam, to say that he was going to stay on in Holland for a day or two, Diana felt a surge of relief. She managed to keep her voice coolly affectionate as she asked how the research was going and to tell him to enjoy himself, and then he rang off.

Diana was dreading his return. Resolved on a policy of ignorance, she was uncertain whether she could maintain this once Rupert was actually home again, exchanging news, playing with the boys, even sharing her bed. The extra days would give her further time to strengthen her determination to keep to herself her knowledge of his affair. Meanwhile, she must go and tell the office of her husband's change of plan.

Jean was at her desk, Tom de Blete in a chair beside it and the agent, a tall, lugubrious young man named Sandy Richmond, hovered by a filing-cabinet in his muddy wellington boots. There was a silence as Diana came in, a silence that suggested to her, with her newly heightened sensitivity, that they must have been talking about Rupert.

'I've just spoken to the duke in Holland,' she told them. 'His research is showing results and he's having to stay on for a bit longer.' She felt rather than saw knowing looks exchanged between Tom and Jean and she hurried on. 'Perhaps, Jean, you'd clear his diary until the end of the week.'

'No problem,' said Jean, looking at the book, 'He doesn't have any engagements anyway.'

Diana frowned. 'But I thought he was down to come to the mayor's dinner in Somersham on Thursday? I'm sure we agreed we'd both have to turn up for that.'

'I accepted for you both,' Jean agreed, 'but Rupert told me last week he'd have to scratch.'

'I see.' Diana took a grip on herself: it wasn't the first time recently that Rupert had shirked public duties, and at least now she knew the reason. 'Well, I'd have been going on my own anyway, so at least I have a good excuse for the duke's absence.'

'When he does come back, I want a word with him — several words.' This, blurted out almost belligerently by the usually taciturn agent, made them all look at him in surprise.

'I mean,' he explained, 'I need to get some decisions.'

'Why, Sandy, what's the problem?' Diana gave him an encouraging smile. The estate was not her province, but the agent sounded as if he had a grievance he needed to air.

'The estate doesn't know where it's going,' the agent grumbled. 'I've been asked to provide facts and figures, both for this year and for the medium term, and if we don't cut the milking herds soon, we'll be in trouble over our quota. I need to know if we're going for sheep, or one of the new crops like lupin seed, or whether we're still interested in deer-farming. And are funds going to be available for a further investment in forestry? The duke's had all the papers on his desk, but I can't get any answers.'

'All right, Sandy, all right.' Diana, laughing, held up her hand to stay him. 'I can't give you your answers: but I can make sure Rupert has some time with you as soon as he's home, and Jean can make a note in his diary. Between us, we'll pin him down for you.'

Diana now left them, forcing another cheerful smile

as she closed the door. Out in the corridor that led back to the Dutch parlour, her heels clicked on the marble floor, echoing emptily into the vaults above her. From the great saloon, she could hear the high-pitched, well-modulated tones of one of the lady guides, dilating on the splendours of the Lely portrait of Effie Gray. While it was out of season, Rockport Place still opened by prior appointment: art-lovers from the United States, guilds of ladies from the Midlands, groups of connoisseurs, were made welcome to the splendours of the house and given refreshment afterwards in Effie Gray's Pantry. They made a useful contribution to the running-costs of the vast palace, which would have had to be heated anyway; but Diana sometimes felt that she never had her home to herself.

She was also aware that she herself was in a way a part of the exhibits. In the early days, she had from time to time tagged along at the back of the tours, eavesdropping on the comments of the visitors: more than once she had heard one lady whisper to another, pointing at the well-dressed guide in her pearls, that surely she must be the duchess herself. Diana, in shabby shirt and jeans, had grinned at the guide and made herself scarce: since then, she made sure that if she did make an appearance, she was dressed for the part, and that the guide was tipped off to exclaim in surprise, as if at a great treat, 'Ah, here *is* Her Grace!'

Back in her sitting-room, Diana felt another wave of solitude sweep over her: it was almost solid, as if she were a fly trapped in a cube of ice. All around her, the house bustled with activity: the conducted tour, the office typewriters clattering away, a constant murmuring from Dobson's domain (though no more breakfast parties, thank goodness), a scholar beavering away in the muniments-room, and Molly Platt busy upstairs in the nurseries. Yet there was no one with whom she could talk, in whom she could confide: for to speak of her knowledge would be to betray Rupert; and whatever he might be up to, she was not going to let him down.

Rupert finally came back to Rockport on Friday evening. Diana was in the night nursery when he arrived: the boys were already tucked up in their diminutive beds and rosy with sleep, but they came to when he sat down between them and chortled with delight at his return. It was a warm scene of domestic happiness. Diana laid her hand on Rupert's shoulder and smiled down at her family; feeling a surge of love, she knew that, for this moment at least, the threatening shadow of Betty Bassano did not fall on him.

Once the boys were coaxed back between their sheets, with the lamps out and the little nightlight glowing, Rupert and Diana went down to the library, where they usually sat when alone. There was a good fire, pots of paper-white narcissus scented the room, and above the carved mantelpiece hung one of Rupert's favourite pictures, a painting of the park at Rockport when newly laid out, by a pupil of Canaletto. Diana made him a strong whisky and soda and they settled back to catch up on each other's news.

'How was Amsterdam?' Diana opened. 'I mean, did you make progress with the rubies?'

'It wasn't very satisfactory,' he told her. 'I spent the first few days being shunted from expert to expert. Eventually I had a session with Professor Bosch, who's by way of being the world's top man on Renascence jewels. He endorsed my research, and he agrees the probability that the stones in the Caracci painting are the rubies: but he won't commit himself on the evidence of the photographs: he needs to examine the stones and their setting.'

'Damn,' said Diana. 'So it's back to square one – to Sheila?'

'It looks that way.' Rupert sighed. His face was

deep-lined, dark with fatigue. 'I looked in to see old Dunhill at the trustees' office on my way through London.'

'Good idea. I'm sure it's better to leave it to Mr Dunhill to extract the rubies from Sheila's claws.'

'You might well say so; but she appears to have stymied even him. He wrote her a stiff letter and asked her to look in at the office for a talk: instead, she sent a note saying she was still too distressed to attend to business: and she would be obliged if any such matters were in future referred to her own lawyer. Old Dunhill was apoplectic at the idea of having to deal with Bangers and Mash.'

'Rupert, what on earth are you talking about?'

'Messrs Hanger & Brash – known to their legal confreres as Bangers and Mash. They are one of the new breed of solicitors: very bright, very smart, with chic offices in Mayfair, and sharp as they come. Not the sort of firm that old Dunhill is accustomed to.'

'Well, he'll have to talk to them.'

'He has. He had what he calls an off-the-record chat with Mr Kevin Brash, and got nowhere. The Brash line is that Her Grace Sheila has no knowledge of any so-called heirlooms, and that any jewels in her possession were *bone fide* gifts from her late husband, thank you very much and good day to you, Mr Dunhill.'

'But surely …' Diana frowned, 'surely we know that the rubies exist, and surely we can prove Sheila is sitting on them?'

'No, we can't.' Rupert sounded weary, as if he was going over old ground. 'You see, we were all rather careless, we never dreamed of signing receipts or anything like that. For instance, when you last wore the necklace, all that happened was that I rang up old Dunhill's secretary, and Colin picked up the box on his way down here. When the ball was over, Colin dropped it back at the office. Nothing was signed for. And I can't see the secretary insisting on my father giving a receipt. So there's no proof.'

'What about the emerald?' Diana persisted. 'We have evidence that Sheila was wearing it a few months ago, here in this house.'

'It's not evidence. All we know is that Dame Elizabeth saw an emerald on Sheila's hand: but the Dame isn't an expert on precious stones, and she couldn't testify in court that it's the same ring she last saw on my grandmother's finger.'

'So Sheila wins?'

'For the moment. Old Dunhill's advice is that there is no point in our going to the law: for one thing, our case is by no means watertight, and for another, the publicity would be horrid. He suggests that we must sit tight and do nothing, waiting until Sheila feels the pinch. But that won't give me access to the rubies; and until I have that, all my work has been for nothing.'

Diana sensed his frustration. She knew how proud he was of his artistic scholarship, and how gratified that the results of his research had been endorsed by the eminent Professor Bosch. But there was nothing she could do to help, so she began to tell him her news, ending up with her plans for the forthcoming dinner party.

'... and,' she concluded, 'I've asked Mrs Bassano. I needed an extra woman, as Colin will be here.'

Rupert looked startled, as he sat up. 'But why Betty? I thought you didn't like her.'

'Rupert, I hardly know her at all, I've only met her once. But you used to pester me to ask her here, and she's been very hospitable to you when you've had to go to Lordstanding to see Sheila, so I thought she'd be an excellent addition to our party.'

'Has she accepted?'

'No, not yet. I gather she's been away.'

Diana was conscious that Rupert was staring hard at

her, so she gave him a bright, guileless smile and added,
'I'm sure she'll come. People seldom refuse an invitation
to Rockport.'

Rupert was still looking taken aback, but luckily there
was a diversion as Molly Platt came in to tell them that
their dinner was ready in the octagonal room. On their
own, the Jordans dined in little state, with just Mrs
Dunt, the gamekeeper's wife, to wait on them. Still, they
kept their conversation general; and once coffee was
over, Rupert announced he was bushed and intended to
go to bed. He headed for his dressing-room.

So Diana slept alone that night. Nor did she enjoy
much rest. A gale was howling down the chimney: the
tall sash windows rattled and somewhere in the distance
a loose shutter banged and crashed. She snuggled into
the pillows but her thoughts would not give her peace;
they drew through the coverts of her mind, flushing out
anxiety after anxiety. Had she taken the right line with
Rupert? Had he guessed she now knew? How could she
hope to compete with Betty Bassano, blessed with
charm, good looks and bottomless wealth? Would the
children sense that something was wrong? It wasn't long
before she had herself reduced to a penniless divorcée,
alone and in rags; and at this stage she sat up, turned on
the light and told herself not to be so silly.

Had they still been living in their old home at
Byegrove, where every creaking floorboard was a
familiar friend, Diana would have gone down to the
kitchen and brewed up a hot drink. But that was
unthinkable in this echoing palace; leaving aside its
unfamiliarity, she might set off some of the alarms and
rouse the whole household. Instead, she reached out for
a beloved book – *Lark Rise to Candleford* – and read
steadily until a glimmer of dawn showed at the windows
and then, suddenly, blessed sleep enveloped her.

At Lordstanding, Betty Bassano was at her desk in the

library, deftly slitting open the envelopes of the mail
that had accumulated during her absence. When she
came to the letter from Diana Jordans, she stared down
at the paper for a long time. It was perfectly courteous
and not in the least out of order that Rupert's wife
should ask her to dinner, and considerate of her to take
the trouble to explain why Betty's house-guest Sheila
could not also be asked. Betty accepted at once; she had
a natural curiosity to take a look both at Rupert's wife
and his home. Besides, an invitation to Rockport was
not to be sneezed at.

There was a stack of business letters to which Betty
now turned. From her first husband, she had learned
how to administer her fortune and with her natural
shrewdness she took an active interest in the manage-
ment of her portfolio. A small office had been set up in
the old butler's pantry and here, once a week, a
secretary came in. The girl could type efficiently
enough, but she didn't know the difference between a
debenture and loan stock, unlike her opposite numbers
in America. This was the first time she had actually
criticised England, she realised: and she decided that if
she was going to stay for good, she would have to look
about for an efficient Girl Friday.

Over her shoulder, Betty heard that Sheila had come
in and was now commanding morning coffee from
Pedro.

'Good morning, my sweet,' she said, coming up to the
desk, 'I trust you had a good night's sleep after all the
excitements of your little escapade?'

Betty ignored the innuendo and replied levelly that
she had slept well. But Sheila was looking down at the
papers.

'Is that a letter from Rockport?' she asked,
recognising the crest.

'Yes, it's from Diana. Its an invitation to dinner.'

'Oh, good.' Sheila looked gratified. 'We have

something to look forward to. And I can wear my new blue brocade.'

'I'm afraid the invitation is for me alone. Diana makes that quite clear. I expect she just needs an extra woman to make up her numbers.'

'How rude.' Sheila pouted. 'Still, I suppose it's all we can expect – she's never known how to behave, and with her background it's hardly surprising.'

The telephone began to ring and Sheila's hand was first to the receiver. It seemed that the call was for her, for she squeaked with delight, agreed enthusiastically to everything said to her and put down the telephone wearing her brightest smile.

'That was Josh, the dear boy,' she explained. 'He's coming down this weekend. That is all right, isn't it, darling?' she added as a concession to her hostess.

'I suppose so.' Sheila's son was not as welcome at Lordstanding as his mother seemed to think. 'But he can't have the blue room this time: I may need that for Christine Sax, if I can prise her out of her suite at Claridge's. And you might warn Joshua that I didn't regard a fifty-penny piece as an adequate tip when last time he brought down his entire wardrobe for poor Maria to wash.'

'I know, he's hopeless.' Sheila gave an indulgent laugh. 'I do feel I have to make it up to the poor boy: his father didn't leave him a bean and I felt I rather neglected him when I was living abroad.'

Betty suspected that her friend's stand against the Jordans trustees was at least in part intended to benefit the wayward Sir Joshua; and this train of thought led her to ask Sheila how her battle with Mr Dunhill was going.

'There's not going to be a battle,' said Sheila, 'at least, not as far as I'm concerned. My new lawyer-man is prepared to be as tough as he needs be, and he will deal with the trustees in future. He takes the line that whatever jewellery I have was a present from Jamey, and it's up to old Mr Dunhill to prove any different. Mr Brash says that even if they could do that, which he doubts, they are unlikely to go to court.'

'But what about the rubies, Sheila? Rupert was told in Amsterdam that he will have to submit them to expert examination before he can prove provenance and the link with that Carracci painting.'

'They can't be that important to him – besides, he has other things to distract him, hasn't he, my sweet?' Sheila was looking arch again. 'Anyway, your precious Rupert will just have to wait until I've screwed what I want out of his trustees.'

'He's not my precious Rupert,' said Betty crisply.

'Not yet, maybe: but I'm sure you're working on it.' With the satisfied air of the one who has the last word, Sheila left the room. Betty could hear her in the hall, asking Pedro to fix her an appointment with the hairdresser in Mallaby and then to bring the car (Betty's car, of course) round.

With a sigh, Betty returned to her papers; but concentration was impossible. Sheila's last remark had left behind a bad taste. Betty did not see herself as a home-breaker: she had seen enough of that in America, where attractive women were ruthless in their pursuit of men with a price tag on them in the hundreds of millions – and vice versa too, she reminded herself ruefully, thinking of her ex. She had entered into her affair with Rupert whole-heartedly: his wiry energy was much to her taste, he was intelligent, considerate, good company; and the days and nights they had spent together in Holland had confirmed that, physically and mentally, they were in tune.

Back in November, they had more or less fallen into bed together: and the affair had proceeded on a casual basis, with continued frank enjoyment and with growing affection. But there had been no calculation about it; for all Sheila's heavy hints, Betty had not thought of herself as a future Duchess of Jordans. She recognised that Rupert had a wife and children to whom he was devoted, and she had learned that he liked to keep the various aspects of his life in separate compartments. His responsibilities as duke were in one such, as a husband and father in another, and there were further pigeon-holes for his other interests, like scholarship in the world of fine art; and now, she guessed, there was a new slot, which she herself occupied, labelled 'mistress'.

Betty was a realist, and the harsh word did not shock her. Nonetheless, for all her independence – both financial and of character – such a subservient role was not one in which she had ever imagined herself. She liked to be a partner to the man in her life, which was why her firt marriage had been such a success and her second a flop.

She recognised that since the trip to Amsterdam, her relationship with Rupert had changed and deepened. But both knew that neither was yet committed wholly to the other; and Betty's growing knowledge of Rupert told her that if they were to take the final leap towards matrimony, a decision that would affect Rupert, his family and his standing, more shattering than it could ever touch her, then it must be up to her. To that extent, Sheila's last comment held true.

And Betty was by no means sure in her own mind that she wanted to be a duchess. In the eyes of the world, in Jackson Hole, Palm Beach and London, it might look like a triumph; but the world did not matter to Rupert. His life was here in Mallamshire, his work and his responsibilities; unlike his father, he would never regard these as well lost for love. Besides, Betty had been living long enough at Lordstanding to learn that in all the many duties that fell to Mallamshire's duchess, Diana Jordans performed to perfection. She would be a tough act to follow.

So, for the moment, she told herself, she would be content to remain in the part of mistress. Because of the need for secrecy, it would be a lonely role; and for the first time, Betty was glad that Sheila had stayed on for so long. After all, Sheila was in the know, and it was good to have a confidante in the house: and Sheila had it in her, Betty remembered, to be a brick when a crisis loomed.

Betty's thoughts were cut into by the telephone. It was Rupert, and after an exchange of their private language of love, he came to the point.

'I meant to ring you sooner,' he was saying, 'but I haven't been able to be on my own until now. Tell me, have you received a letter from Diana?'

'An invitation to dinner? Yes, I have. Why?'

'You'll refuse, of course.' It was not a question.

'Certainly not,' she replied. 'In fact, I have already accepted.'

'Well, you can't have posted it yet. You really must not think of coming here.'

'Oh, come off it, Rupert.' She knew what the trouble was: she would be hopping from one pigeon-hole into the next. 'It's very kind of Diana to ask me. And for me to appear at her dinner table is the perfect cover: it means that nobody can suspect anything is going on between us.'

'I hope you're right.' He didn't sound convinced, but went on to suggest dinner that night. 'There's a very good pub over at Bellowing: we might head there for a change.'

Bellowing was on the other side of the county, a long way from the usual haunts of Rupert and his friends. Betty realised what was in his mind, and for a moment she hesitated, reluctant to be slotted into the secret drawer reserved for mistresses; but he sounded so eager that she soon gave in.

Eleven

On the evening of her dinner party, Diana Jordans was at her dressing-table. Around her, she could feel the great house was in a state of hushed anticipation, like a theatre before curtain-up. Rupert was in his bath, the boys were tucked up in bed, Molly Platt had all under control in her kitchen, with two women from the village to assist, Dobson and James were seeing to the wines. The engine of Rockport Place was tuned up, ticking over smoothly to provide its stately best for the twenty guests to come.

That things were running so smoothly was due to the new-found amity between the 'old staff' and Molly's kitchen. Diana was still surprised that her firm stand with Dobson had paid off so well: instead of being obstructive, Dobson was now on the side of his new chatelaine. Only this morning, when Diana had poked her head into the state dining-room to see Dobson and James hard at work laying out the glittering display of Paul Storr, not for the edification of the paying visitors but for the use of proper guests, Dobson had made the final *amende honorable*.

'Will Your Grace be requiring canapés this evening?' he enquired. 'Some of Mrs Platt's celebrated vol-au-vents perhaps? If so, I shall instruct James accordingly.'

Diana had given him a steady look. Both of them were remembering the Christmas party, when James, out of malice or through forgetfulness, had failed to circulate

Molly's contribution. She smiled at the old butler in understanding and told him that Molly was much too busy but perhaps Mrs Smiles might make some of her excellent cheese straws.

To have gained the respect of Dobson gave Diana confidence: and it was confidence she would need tonight. She was well accustomed to receiving a variety of guests into her home, to making them at ease and bringing out their best; but this evening Betty Bassano was to be present. Diana always took trouble over her appearance, although she was one of those fortunate beings who look neat and pretty even at their lowest: tonight she had chosen a low-cut dress in crimson brocade, which showed off her creamy shoulders and slender neck. She had originally bought the dress to complement the Rockport rubies, she remembered; but this evening was not an occasion for a full display of the ducal heirlooms, even had the rubies been available; instead, she chose a small diamond star, a present from Rupert to mark the birth of their first son.

She leaned forward into the mirror to examine her appearance closely. Her dark hair, set into soft waves that framed her heart-shaped face, shone smoothly; but that very morning her hairdresser had found the first grey at her temples (now eliminated by his artifice) and she could see in her reflection staring back at her that there was a taut wariness about her eyes and even a few fatal wrinkles upon her clear brow. She applied herself to her make-up box to do something about the wrinkles.

As her fingers worked away, she was running over in her mind her seating-plan. The day before, Rupert had come across her in the Dutch parlour, surrounded by discarded diagrams and frowning.

'That wretched wife of the High Sheriff has cried off because of 'flu,' she told him. 'It's put my table-plan into chaos.'

'Why, are we a woman short?'

'No, your mother has rallied to the cause, bless her. But now we have so many family, it's a nightmare trying to spread us all around the table.'

'Let's have a look.' Rupert leaned over her shoulder to study the latest plan. 'I say,' he protested, 'you've landed poor Betty Bassano with the general. It's her first dinner here: we ought to give her a better place.'

It was so unlike Rupert to interfere in Diana's arrangements that she rected sharply.

'Mrs Bassano will have to sing for her supper like everyone else. Besides, she has Colin on her other side.' And she added as a tease, 'Perhaps he'll fall for her. That would be satisfactory, don't you think? All those lovely dollars secured to your brother!'

But Rupert had turned away, and she hadn't been able to observe his reaction.

Noises next door now told her that Rupert had finished his bath. It would soon be time for them to gather in the library for a quiet drink before their guests arrived. They had always enjoyed this brief moment together, making bets as to who would be the first to arrive, discussing who might be a little shy and need bringing out. She bent to attach the diamond droplet ear-rings that would complete her toilette.

In his dressing-room, Rupert was also at a mirror, carefully tying his black bow tie. He was in high good spirits: he enjoyed his own dinner parties, he enjoyed displaying the treasures of his house to his guests, and this evening was to be given a special piquancy with Betty's presence. The hole-in-the-corner secrecy of their affair give it a special relish, and they would share a conspiracy of delight amid an unknowing crowd, catching an eye, exchanging a quick half-smile.

A tap at the door broke into his thoughts. It was his brother Colin.

'I'm sorry to burst in you like this,' he was saying, 'but I needed to have a word with you, and I have to get back to town in the morning.'

'What's up, Colin?' Rupert was brushing down the collar of his dinner jacket.

'There was a meeting of the trustees yesterday,' his brother told him, 'and we spent a good deal of time on the subject of the missing heirlooms.'

'Why bother? From what old Dunhill told me, I understood that there wasn't to be any immediate action.'

'Old Dunhill isn't the only trustee: and on this occasion, his view did not prevail.' Colin sounded pleased with himself. 'It has now been decided that the trustees will instruct solicitors to proceed against Sheila, Duchess of Jordans for the recovery of all property of the trustees presently believed to be in her keeping.'

'God, you sound pompous, Colin.' Rupert was irritated that a major policy decision had been taken without his prior knowledge.

'Maybe, but we really can't let that greedy little Sheila get away with the rubies. And you do want them back, don't you, Rupert?'

'Of course I do. I need them in my hands before I can complete my work. I just don't think this is the right way to go about their recovery. Besides, old Dunhill was pretty doubtful that we had hard proof that Sheila actually has the damned things.'

'We are satisfied we have enough proof to start proceedings. And we believe that once the story hits the headlines, it will make it impossible for Sheila to flog her loot. No reputable dealer would touch the stuff.'

'There are plenty of less reputable men, I'm afraid. And meanwhile, we will all suffer from the most ghastly press. Sheila will make the most of her interviews, and I'll be painted as a rapacious son trying to do down his father's widow. Not nice.' Rupert turned to face his brother. 'And goodness knows what else a good reporter might dig up once his attention is focused on us. Had you thought of that?' Rupert looked very worried indeed.

'If you've nothing to hide, you've nothing to fear. Strictly speaking, you're not involved in the legal battle at all: it's all a matter for the trustees and you can remain aloof.'

'You can say that easily enough, Colin, but you know as well as I do that I'll be the focus of all eyes, that I'll be persecuted with photographers and inaccurate stories. I'll be facing the music, and I do think I ought to have been consulted.'

'I'm sorry, Rupert.' Colin shrugged. 'The decision has been made, and I was asked to communicate it to you.'

Lord Colin left his brother scowling into his mirror. The earlier bonhomie had flown, leaving Rupert angry and anxious. Sheila had a nasty little temper when roused, he knew, and she was quite capable of dropping a few salacious hints about her stepson's private life. Once heavy hints about Betty appeared in, say, *Private Eye*, Diana would be badly hurt. And there were the boys to consider, too. All in all, Rupert felt that events were running away outside his control, and he decided he would go down to his business-room and have a stiff whisky before facing the party.

So when Diana entered the Library, she found only Colin there. He told her he was glad to have the chance of a word on their own, and he went on to tell her of the trustees' decision to take Sheila to court.

'I'll tip you the wink when the story's about to break,' he said, 'and I'm afraid you may have a few difficult days with the reporters.'

'Have you told Rupert? What does he have to say?'

'I'm afraid he's a bit miffed he wasn't involved; but we think it's much better to keep both of you well out of the line of fire.'

'I understand that,' said Diana, 'and I suppose it will be worth it if we can get the jewels back. I take it the trustees have a cast-iron case?'

Colin's thin face looked a little wary.

'Between ourselves, it's not watertight,' he admitted, 'but at least we consider we'll be stopping Sheila from flogging off the heirlooms on the side. But' – he broke off to look down at Diana's resolute and pretty face – 'you might be able to help the case.'

'I'll be glad to lend a hand,' she told him. 'Rupert is very frustrated that he can't get hold of the rubies and I'd love to be a party to getting them back for him.'

'Well then: will you cast your mind around and think if you know of anybody who has seen Sheila wearing any of the jewels in the past few years?'

'Oh dear, that's quite beyond me, I'm afraid. We don't know any of Sheila's friends.'

'There must be someone,' said Colin. 'Sheila's not the sort to hide her spoils away – she must have flaunted 'em somewhere. Think about it, Diana: and if you do come up with a possible witness, let me know. It would also be wiser,' he added cautiously, 'if you didn't tell Rupert.'

'I can't promise that,' Diana said sharply. Colin's request sounded like an aspersion of her loyalty to her husband.

'I'm not asking you to do anything behind Rupert's back – just not to tell him if you should come across any evidence that might help us.'

Colin could say no more; Dobson had flung open the double doors and taken up station.

'Major-General and Mrs Makepeace,' he announced in a mighty voice.

Diana hurried forward, her hostess's smile of welcome pinned to her face, hiding her inner disappointment that she hadn't been able to place her bet on the military punctuality of the general and his lady.

The next to arrive were Lord and Lady Mallaby.

They were old and trusted friends, and Diana was glad to have them by her before Mrs Bassano made her entrance; by this time, Rupert had joined his guests and made much of Angela Mallaby, whose fair English looks were enhanced by a simple dress in cornflower blue that echoed her deep eyes and made her look, as he told her with gallantry, more like a girl of twenty than a respectable mother and marchioness to boot.

Now the guests were arriving in a steady stream and Diana was kept busy with greetings and introductions. Soon, her head-count told her that only three were still to come: and one of these was Betty.

'Sir Henry and Lady Luckton and Mrs Bassano,' Dobson trumpeted into the gathering.

Consuelo Luckton was renowned as a Spanish American of great and lustrous beauty; but tonight it was on Betty Bassano that all eyes turned. She was wearing a severely cut long dress in flaming scarlet, with a high Chinese collar and very full Mandarin sleeves; her tawny hair was swept up smoothly, leaving her neck bare, and her only jewellery was a heavily chased gold chain that looped around her waist. Betty's appearance breathed high fashion and Diana, approaching, felt suddenly small and drab in her dark brocade.

She greeted both Lucktons and then turned to the last guest.

'I'm so glad to welcome you to Rockport at last,' she said, smiling and holding out her hand. 'I know you've been so kind to Rupert when he's been seeing his stepmother and we're both very grateful.'

Looking up into Betty's face, with its high cheekbones and scarlet lips, Diana saw in her eyes a wariness, even a tick of nerves. She felt better as Betty replied in her husky voice that she was very grateful for the invitation. Tucking her arm into Betty's, Diana led her firmly round the room for punctilious introduction; and she was surprised to find how many of the company already knew the newcomer and greeted her effusively. Even the Lord Lieutenant, twinkling behind his white moustache, had a memory of Betty as a gawky teenager riding out from Wrighton Manor to attend the pony club.

Diana left them together: she sensed rather than saw that Rupert was approaching, and she had no wish to be a too-brightly-smiling witness of their greeting.

Dinner proceeded smoothly and by the time the venison was handed round, Diana began to feel she could relax. Under the direction of Dobson's eyebrows, the wines were circulating: conversation seemed animated, with no one left on their own. Betty Bassano, she noted with approval, had done her duty stalwartly with her right-hand neighbour the general, who had now turned to Lorna Jordans, leaving Betty to Colin. Both seemed to be enjoying themselves, and Diana herself turned to concentrate on the judge on her left.

'I appreciate, my dear duchess,' he was saying, 'that there are many demands on your time; so I hope you will forgive me for suggesting yet another.'

'I'll always help if I can,' she told him, 'but my diary gets pretty full. What have you in mind?' She assumed it was another fête or function.

'I was talking to the chairman of Somersham Petty Sessions the other day,' the judge explained, 'and it appears that there is an unexpected shortage of justices on his bench. It is always difficult to achieve a balanced bench, and he's on the look-out for some possible names – suitable names, of course – from the country-dwellers.'

'As a magistrate, do you mean? I should have thought, Judge, there was no shortage of candidates.'

'There's often a shortage of people with the right motives, Duchess. Officially, appointments are nothing to do with me – they lie in the hands of the local committee who make recommendations to the Lord Chancellor: but I have been asked to take soundings.'

'Judge, are you sounding me out?' Diana was taken

aback: she had never thought of herself as a potential Justice of the Peace.

'It is a commitment,' he admitted. 'Apart from training sessions, you would expect to sit at least every fortnight – probably more – and there are various committees and panels on which you might also play a part. It is,' he added, 'very interesting work and very worth while.'

'I'm sorry.' Diana shook her head. 'I'm tempted, but I have too much to do here already, and I don't spend enough time with my children as it is.'

'Rockport's gain is justice's loss,' he said with elaborate courtesy. 'Still, if you should happen to think of any suitable candidates, I would be most obliged to hear of them.'

'I will see what I can do,' she told him; and with that the judge was content; for, along with the rest of Mallamshire, he knew that once the Duchess of Jordans undertook a task, it was as good as done.

At the end of dinner, Diana signalled to withdraw the ladies. She adhered to the custom less to afford the men the opportunity to take port and talk politics or dirt than to give the party a shake-up, with the practical advantage of access to the lavatories.

Coffee was to be served in the green drawing-room. Here, under the glittering chandeliers and with the braided ropes that usually herded tourists down their appointed path tidied away, was a huge log fire; banks of potted lilies stood around and on the walls the famous Bellini and the vast Caravaggio glowed. None of the women stayed here, all the same; those who didn't wish to avail themselves of the bathrooms or Diana's dressing-table still hoped that they might have a chance to view the private apartments, to see for themselves with what ingenuity and taste modern comforts had been contrived within the fabric of the mansion.

The oak stairs, though sumptuously carved, were not

wide: they ascended two by two and Betty Bassano found herself in step with Rupert's mother Lorna, whom she had met for the first time before dinner. The elder duchess, as tall as Betty and elegant in silver satin, had been distant, even frosty; so, determined to break the ice, Betty prattled away as they mounted the stairs. When they reached the galleried landing, she pointed at the still spuriously labelled Caravaggio that hung above a bulbous French commode.

'Isn't it thrilling about that painting?' she said. 'Rupert's done a wonderful job in tracing its provenance and proving it's a Carracci.'

'Indeed?' Lorna's tone was very cold. 'That's my son's business and I'm afraid I never discuss family affairs with strangers.'

With that, she turned and disappeared behind a door that led to the nurseries, where she hoped to have a glimpse of her sleeping grandsons.

Betty was left aghast; but then she was swept up by Consuelo Luckton and Caro Brinscomb, who were in fits of laughter at some joke, and they took her off to one of the spare rooms.

From her place at the rear of the party, Diana had observed the exchange between her mother-in-law and Betty. It was very unlike Lorna to be rude. It must mean that Lorna had wind of what was going on and, despite Betty's obvious attractions, disapproved. For a moment, Diana was glad, relieved to find that she had at least one ally in her lonely war. But she felt too a twinge of regret that one of her guests had experienced the rough side of Lorna's tongue: she must try to make public amends.

On the landing were the judge's wife and the Lord Lieutenant's lady, their eyes expectant as those of labradors beseeching a treat. Diana knew what they wanted, and took them off on a conducted tour of the first floor. She was by now quite accustomed to showing people around her private quarters: it meant a lot to them (and gave them much fodder for talk in the world outside). Nor did she resent such invasion of her home: she was often conscious of a sense of privilege that she lived in such a vast palace, with its staff and its countless treasures, and she enjoyed the sense of sharing it all with others.

They finished the tour in the nursery kitchen, where they found Lorna talking to the village girl who had recently, on Molly Platt's recommendation, taken charge as Nanny. Diana arranged that her mother-in-law would escort the other ladies back down to the green drawing-room, as she wanted to look in on the boys. After that, she decided to make use of her own bathroom before rejoining the party.

She opened her bedroom door. Betty was there, seated at the stood in front of the dressing-table, her scarlet skirt spread out around her. For an instant, Diana felt as if she was spinning out of time and into a black hole: the scene was like a tableau of the future, showing Betty in her bedroom, at her dressing-table, in possession and with Diana herself no longer in existence. Was this how it was to be?

She could not speak. But she must have made some noise, for Betty looked up and saw her.

'I'm terribly sorry,' she was saying, having seen the shock in Diana's face, 'but the other bathroom was very crowded so Angela Mallaby brought me in here while I fix my hair. She said it would be all right.'

'Of course it's all right.' Diana found her voice and forced it to be calm. 'And I hope you've found everything you need.'

The two women looked at each other across the room. Betty was smiling; it seemed a tentative, appeasing expression, and Diana was suddenly aware of a need to talk, directly, without the barriers of politeness and yet without rancour, to this obviously attractive, generous and intelligent woman.

Betty, it appeared, felt something of the same, for she began to move towards Diana, her hands outstretched: and then Angela emerged from the bathroom. Evidently, she sensed something of the tension between the other two, for she suggested with a briskness that was unusual for her that by now the men must have left the dining-room, and together they went downstairs.

As they entered the green drawing-room, Diana saw that the rest of the party was re-assembled. James the footman was circulating coffee, Dobson drinks, and several of the men were armed with cigars. Rupert was standing by the fireplace beside his mother, and they both looked hard across the room at the group by the door. Remembering her wish to atone for Lorna's attitude, Diana again took Betty's arm in the most friendly fashion and took her across to a group that included Colin and Henry Luckton. Then, satisfied that Betty was happily ensconced with kindred spirits, and managing to avoid catching Rupert's eye, she resumed her hostly duties.

The more elderly members of the gathering did not stay late. There was a determined effort by the younger element, led by Caro Brinscomb and Henry Luckton, to prolong the occasion, but Dobson's beetling eyebrows did their work and soon the host and hostess were left alone.

In the past, this had been the time when Rupert and Diana took a last drink and picked over together the evening; but tonight Rupert seemed unwilling to say much. His replies to Diana's remarks were monosyllabic, and when she said brightly what a success Betty Bassano had been, he gave her one quick, suspicious look before suggesting that she looked tired and why didn't she go to bed.

'I'll just do the rounds with the night watchman,' he said, 'and then I'll be upstairs.'

Much later, Diana was in bed, half-asleep and with the

lights out. A shaft of light came through from Rupert's dressing-room: dimly, she heard him creep in and close the door.

Twelve

The last of the departing guests emerged on to the perron under the portico of Rockport Place. It was a cold, clear night, with the stars bright against a black sky, and they stood for a moment, looking down to the lake where a soft mist lay like a handkerchief across the still water. Confronted by the sudden chill, Joe Brinscomb staggered and grasped the stone balustrade to steady himself.

'Darl, you're pissed,' said his wife sharply, her Australian accent cutting the winter air. 'And I'm not going to drive home either.'

Caro Brinscomb, swathed in mink, was a short young woman with the features of a pretty piglet. She was very confident of her attractions and had the sleek, plump look of someone who was used to having her cake and eating it.

'Don't worry,' Henry Luckton intervened. 'You can leave your car here. We can easily take you home to Harvestone after we've dropped Betty off at Lordstanding.'

So it was arranged, and they all piled into the Lucktons' roomy Range Rover. Harvestone was the ancestral home of the Brinscombs: Joe was of a cadet branch that had made its fortune in Australia and returned to Mallamshire a few years back, supplanting his cousin the present Lord Brinscomb who had, however, thwarted Caro's social ambitions by producing a baby son and heir.

Caro's antennae were acute, and she lost no time in declaring her interest as soon as they had left off Betty.

'Wasn't Betty terrific tonight,' she said from the back of the car. 'It must have taken the hell of a nerve to walk into Diana's drawing-room as bold as brass.'

'She looked a million dollars,' Joe put in. 'The old fogies couldn't take their eyes off her.'

'Especially by comparison with Diana.' Caro was showing her hand. 'The poor little thing looked positively dowdy.'

'I think it was very courteous of Diana not to try to outshine her guests,' Consuelo lisped quietly. She liked to see the good in everyone. 'Still, she did not look her best – she seemed tired and strained.'

'Hardly surprising,' Joe commented from beside his wife, 'when Rupe the duke is playing around with the lovely Betty all over the country. Good luck to him, that's what I say.'

'I wonder if Diana knows what is going on?' asked Consuelo.

'She can't,' said Caro flatly. 'Even she wouldn't be such a sucker as to ask her rival to flaunt herself in her own drawing-room.'

'Diana is not a fool, I think,' Consuelo said. 'Perhaps she doesn't mind about Betty.'

'Could be,' Henry Luckton put in from the wheel. 'Grandees have never given much importance to such trivia as marital fidelity.'

'But that's the point,' said Caro. 'Diana isn't a grandee at all – she's only the daughter of a pub-keeper when all's said and done. Betty will make a smashing duchess, if you ask me: my money's on her.'

'… and it's her money that'll clinch it for Rupert, you wait and see.' Joe gave a coarse laugh. 'No duke could resist all those lovely dollars.'

'So,' Caro crowed gleefully, 'it's Betty for Duchess of

Jordans!' Caro liked to be on the winning side: and she had been quick to consolidate her friendship with the newly arrived Mrs Bassano.

'I'm not sure that I agree with you.' Henry Luckton spoke slowly. In part, he was concentrating on the road ahead, which involved some narrow bends: but also, he was aware that of the four of them, he was the only one who was truly Mallamshire. Lucktons had farmed their land at Luckton Malford for two hundred years, and although Henry had played little social part in the county until his spectacular marriage, he had a feeling for the community in which they all lived.

'Diana works very hard,' he pointed out. 'She serves on all sorts of committees, and she's always willing to lend a hand to a good cause. Somehow, I can't see Betty in that role.'

'She wouldn't have to.' Caro's tone was that of someone who has worked everything out. 'It won't have escaped your notice that Rupert hasn't yet sold Byegrove, where they lived before he succeeded. I'll bet he's planning to instal Diana there with the boys: she can carry on with her good works and then he and Betty can whoop it up at Rockport. Betty gives terrific parties – far better than that stuffy dinner we've just endured.'

Henry made no reply. As a working farmer he had to be up early, and he was anxious to be home and to bed. With relief, therefore, they dropped the Brinscombs at Harvestone and drove off into the night.

On the morning after, Angela and Andrew Mallaby were having breakfast at the Manor of Braye. Sunlight streamed in, and there was the appetising smell of coffee in the air, while a bowl of cheerful yellow crocuses brought promise that spring was not far off. Andrew was deep in *The Times*, leaving Angela to her thoughts as she crumbled a piece of toast.

She had no appointments for the day ahead. That was

good: and she remembered the Chinese proverb that to be at leisure for one whole day is to be for one day immortal. There was nothing untoward in the post, their two sons upstairs were in high spirits, and her teenage daughter Rosemary, who tended to be an uncomfortable and disruptive influence on the household, was safely absent at an art school in London.

Yet Angela was worried. She hadn't at all liked what she had seen last night at Rockport. Both Diana and Rupert Jordans were old friends; Rupert she had known off and on all her life, and when he had first produced his pretty girl-friend at the Manor of Braye, Angela had taken to her at once. With the rumours rife about Rupert and the newcomer Betty Bassano, it had been a shock to find Betty an honoured guest at Diana's table. And Angela had not failed to notice how well Betty seemed to be established among the other guests, how attractive, gregarious and out-going was her easy manner.

After nearly ten years, the Mallabys' own marriage was rock solid, with foundations of deep love and trust. Now approaching fifty, she felt that they were approaching the sunlit uplands, where what anxieties they had would be faced together and within their abilities. She wasn't in the least smug; but she was apt to think that the married state was the best that this world had to offer; and she was shaken to discover that Diana's marriage, which she had thought as safe as her own, looked in danger.

With a slow and loving smile, she looked across the table. Andrew caught her eye and, returning the smile, he folded his newspaper and laid it beside his plate.

'I know that look,' he said in his rich, deep voice. 'You're brooding. And I'd guess you're worrying about Diana Jordans. You really mustn't: for one thing, it's none of our business, and for another, Diana is a very capable young woman and fully equipped to deal with her own problems.'

His lean, dark face, with deep sardonic lines etched on

either side of his long nose, seemed to offer reassurance; but this she refused to accept.

'I can't think what can have got into Rupert's head,' she said. 'He's always been so loving towards Diana, and he adores the boys. He can't want to hurt her.'

'I'm sure he doesn't. He's probably just feeling his oats. After all, he hasn't been a duke for very long. I expect he thinks its rather buckish to have a mistress on the side – like one of his eighteenth-century forebears.'

'That might have been all very well then, but I don't believe Diana would see Rupert's behaviour in that way. Do you think she knows what's going on?'

'I wouldn't think so. Diana received Mrs Bassano very affectionately last night.'

'And wasn't Mrs Bassano a success? Everyone in the county appears to have taken to her.'

'I like her,' Andrew pointed out mildly.

'Oh, so do I. What I don't like is the thought she may become Rupert's second duchess. After all, she's loaded with dollars, and if she has social ambitions, she couldn't be aiming much higher.'

'That may be: but it's no concern of ours.'

'Yes, it is,' Angela insisted. 'We're both devoted to Rupert and Diana, and I don't want to see them break up. You wouldn't consider having a word with Rupert on the quiet?'

'No, I would not,' said Andrew with horror. 'I couldn't possibly interfere.'

'Maybe not – but I might have a girl's chat with Diana.'

'Much better not.' Andrew was crisply firm. He was remembering how, years ago, Angela had taken on much the same task with Lorna, when Jamie Jordans was first entangled with Sheila. As he recalled, it hadn't done much good; and he had the firm masculine conviction that the state of a marriage was for the parties concerned and for no one else.

'I wish,' Angela was going on, 'I wish we could show Diana we're on her side, at least. If she's not careful, she's going to find herself quite isolated.' Then, realising that her husband wasn't going to offer much help, she made up her mind on another course of action.

'I think I'll go and have a chat with Bessie de Blete.'

If Angela's intention was to bring Dame Elizabeth up to date with events at Rockport Place, she was forestalled. The Dame had been pottering about her garden, wrapped in a vast blue quilted coat against the blustering March wind that was battering an early clump of daffodils when, looking over her wall, she saw Molly Platt walking across the village green. She waved and beckoned Molly over, for she had a great affection for the girl, having taken her and her small love-child under her protection when Molly first returned to Braye, abandoned by her lover.

Molly came over, and the Dame bustled her into the warm kitchen where she brewed a pot of tea. Molly was explaining that it was her day off from Rockport and she had been on her way from seeing her grandfather, old Gabriel, to pay a visit on her auntie who lived on the council estate above the green.

'But I'm right glad to see you, Miss, really I am,' Molly concluded as the Dame sat down opposite her at the kitchen table.

Molly's round, scrubbed face was showing an anxiousness that the Dame knew of old, and she set to probe out the problem.

'Young Elvis all right?' she asked breezily; not that she was much interested in those beneath an age where their problems might involve her, but she knew of Molly's devotion to her son. The reply was positive: the boy loved his school and seemed very happy at Rockport.

'And how are you getting on with the old staff at the big house?' the Dame tried again. 'Are you still in mortal fear of Dobson's eyebrows?'

'Well now, Miss, that is the most extraordinary thing.' Molly set down her cup with a clatter and leaned forward to explain. 'They were all real nasty to me at first, ever so haughty and cold – quite unkind, really.'

Dame Elizabeth made a sympathetic noise. For the gentle Molly, 'unkind' was an uncommonly strong word.

'But recently, they've all changed,' Molly went on. 'I think Miss Diana squared up to Mr Dobson and told him what for; anyway, ever since, she can do no wrong in his eyes: and what Mr Dobson says goes for Mrs Smiles and old James too. Now they are for ever inviting me into their kitchen for cups of tea and slices of cake. And my goodness, Miss, how they talk!'

'You musn't let that worry you, Molly. In a big house like Rockport, the servants always know exactly what is going on.'

'You've put your finger on it, Miss. They're saying the most dreadful things about Mr Rupert – I mean, His Grace. I don't like talking out of turn, Miss, but you're a friend of Miss Diana's, and I think you ought to know what is being said.'

'And what is that?' The Dame probed again.

'Well, Miss, they're saying that His Grace is carrying on with another lady. Name of Mrs Basin, or something like that, and from all accounts stinking rich. And last night I saw her, bold as brass, sitting at Miss Diana's dining-table.'

Dame Elizabeth was astonished. 'Are you telling me that Mrs Bassano dined last night at Rockport?'

'That's right,' Molly nodded, satisfied by the Dame's reaction to her news, 'just as if she was proper county. And Mr Dobson says she was ever so confident and made a great hit with all the gentlemen.'

Dame Elizabeth fell silent, assembling her thoughts.

If Betty Bassano had been an honoured guest at Rockport, had Diana acted on her own in issuing the invitation, or had Rupert been callous enough to suggest that his wife entertain his mistress? On the face of it, it seemed unlikely; but the Dame knew Diana to be both intelligent and clear-headed: she might well have resolved on a policy of determined ignorance. Such a line had not worked for Rupert's mother when Jamey Jordans first dallied with Sheila Fiske; and the Dame didn't think it would succeed with Rupert either. But even Dame Elizabeth was loth to interfere in a rocky marriage: the odium of all parties concerned was the only likely outcome. She would have to wait, she decided, until and if she herself was approached for advice. So she turned the conversation to the subject of Gabriel Platt's health, which kept them both occupied until Molly rose to depart and the Dame returned to her wind-blown garden.

Rupert Duke of Jordans, the subject of all this speculation, was meanwhile driving to Lordstanding. He was quite unaware that his affair with Betty was in the public domain; and if he had known, he would only have cared if word reached his wife. He loved Diana as he loved his sons: they were his family and a main part of his life. But, always provided Diana was not hurt, he did not feel that he was in any way betraying her; and, without articulating the thought, he sensed vaguely that his position and his rank insulated him from the rigours of conventional *mores*.

Betty had telephoned that morning, to say that Sheila had taken herself to London for the day. With the coast clear, he headed for Lordstanding at once, chucking a long-standing engagement with the land agent (a decision about deer-farming had still to be made).

Rupert was taking the back road that led under the Downs. As his car breasted a rolling green rampart, he paused. Spread before him was the panorama of the upper reaches of the river Mal, its fields and farmsteads dappled under the running shadows cast by the tattered clouds. Behind him lay the thousands of acres of the Rockport estates, with the Palladian mansion and its lake shrouded in a sudden shower; and before him, just beyond the market town of Mallaby, he could see Lordstanding sitting on its bluff above the river, its handsome facade turned to ochre by a shaft of sunlight.

The prospect seemed to symbolise Rupert's life at this moment. Rockport represented care, anxiety, heavy responsibility: to his worries about the estate and the ever-mounting costs of maintaining the palace that was his heritage was added his frustration at not being able to complete his work on the Carracci painting and his fear that the trustees might not be successful in retrieving the Rockport rubies, now so crucial to that work. Another fear arose from the impending court case against his stepmother: Sheila, after all, was one of the few people privy to the secret of his affair with Betty, and she was quite capable, out of spite if not for direct advantage, of blurting out what she knew.

He knew, from Betty's telephone call, that Sheila had heard that morning from her solicitor and had decided upon an immediate trip to London to confer with him. That suggested that the trustees had now made their move, that the law-suit was under way: that meant trouble: trouble from the press, trouble to protect Diana and the boys, and, most dangerous of all, trouble from Sheila.

About the state of his marriage, Rupert resolutely refused to think. He was aware, without articulating the thought, that his relationship with Diana was changing; but that was inevitable after nearly ten years together: he still loved her and admired her, but desire had died. All his energies in that respect were devoted to Betty.

Betty was attractive and generous both of mind and

body. They shared many interests; but above all, she made him laugh. And there hadn't been much laughter in his life recently: the burden of his position in the county grew daily heavier and heavier upon his thin shoulders. He was aware, too, that being a duke wasn't all strawberry leaves: since he had succeeded, people seemed to behave differently to him, and expect him to be different, in some way set apart from the rest of humanity. If he ever forgot, Diana was always ready to remind him of what was expected: dutiful herself, she was quite sharp with him when he last cut an engagement with the agent. He, in turn, was still irritated that she had invited Betty to Rockport without consulting him; it rankled that she thus ignored the frontiers he had so carefully erected between the territories of his life.

So it was with a bubbling access of high spirits, like a schoolboy unexpectedly released from class, that he released the brake and coasted down the hill towards sun-bathed Lordstanding, where he might expect to forget his worries and his obligations in Betty's entrancing company.

Thirteen

Just before Easter, Diana Jordans was driving home from Shipston-on-Mal. She had been there to open a show of local paintings, and after patiently being photographed with a sculptor, a local lady water-colourist and the town mayor, had accepted a glass of sweet sherry with every sign of enthusiasm and embarked on a tour of the gallery, chatting to as many people as possible and – provided she had met them before – getting the names right. It was the sort of thing she did well and enjoyed, even if at times when chatting and bringing people out, she felt as if she was in a glass case labelled 'Duchess: Handle with Care'. Still, it was human contact of a kind, and this was what she needed: these days, she was inclined to suffer waves of loneliness that she found increasingly difficult to damp down.

As she turned on to the bypass, the rain began. No April shower this, it was a heavy downpour that covered the windscreen in solid water and drummed on the car's roof. Cocooned inside, with the demister roaring, she felt her solitude more than ever. If only there were someone with whom she could talk; but friends were out, even close and loving friends like Angela Mallaby, for to confide her secret fears would be a betrayal of Rupert: and with her parents at the Rockport Arms, she was on affectionate but not intimate terms – her mother would be tearfully horrified at the knowledge that all was not well within the marriage of her daughter the duchess, and was, moreover, incapable of holding her tongue.

Then, peering through the storm, she saw the sign showing the turn to the village of Braye, and on an impulse she swung off the main road and down to the green. Braye was the home of the Mallabys: but it was also where Bessie de Blete lived, and Diana remembered she had some business to discuss with the Dame. Besides, there was nothing to hurry home to: the boys were still at school and Rupert had disappeared again – to Lordstanding, she supposed.

Dame Elizabeth was busy at her desk and, she said at once, delighted at the interruption, for she had only been engaged on her monthly bout of paying the bills. Almost in one movement, she made Diana welcome, bustled the cat off the chair by the fire, taken her guest's damp headscarf to dry and, while Diana was still shaking out her hair, had the kettle on and was brewing coffee.

Diana broached the county matter first: it was the most impersonal. She related to the Dame what the judge had said at her dinner party about the need for some new magistrates.

'I simply can't take it on myself,' she said, 'but I knew you'd have some names up your sleeve.'

The Dame was delighted: this was just the sort of job she relished, and as she filtered the coffee, she was riffling through the mental filing-cabinets of her capacious memory.

'Somersham, did you say?' she asked over her shoulder. 'The chairman is George Rafter, he must be getting on a bit. I did hear they were getting too many justices from the town, and not enough from the surrounding areas.'

'The judge told me they needed a balanced bench, whatever that may be.'

'He meant that the justices should represent all

sections of the community,' said the Dame formally. 'The difficulty arises from the amalgamation of courts. In the old days, the smaller towns like Shipston and Mallaby had their own courts, with their own local beaks. But nowadays, it's all concentrated at Somersham; and they are probably short of people from outside the town.'

'Have you any ideas?' asked Diana. 'I had wondered about Christopher Miles.'

Mr Miles was a writer who also lived in Braye; but the Dame soon dismissed his candidature.

'Christopher might indeed make a good JP,' she said, 'but I fancy from what the judge said that the need is for a woman. And in that case, I think it might be appropriate to suggest Angela Mallaby.'

'Angela?' Diana was surprised. 'I love her dearly, but she always seems so wrapped up in her family ...'

'I've known Angela since she was a little girl,' said the Dame, 'and I know her to be fair-minded, level-headed and intelligent.'

'I'm sure she doesn't know a thing about the law.'

'She doesn't need to. The justices have a learned clerk to keep them on the right track on legal matters. I think Angela would make a very good magistrate. Besides, the boys are growing up now, soon they'll be off to school, and it's time Angela made a contribution to the world outside the walls of the Manor of Braye.'

'Then you think I should mention Angela's name to the judge?'

'That's not the way to go about it,' said the Dame. 'You leave it to me: first, I'll sound out Angela, and if she's willing I'll have a quiet word with George Rafter. It's rather a delicate process.'

Diana nodded: she knew that a delicate process was just what the Dame excelled at, and she could relax, confident that her pledge to the judge was redeemed.

The Dame looked closely across at Diana's heart-shaped face. The jaw line was as strong, determined, as ever, and the dark eyes were steadfast; but there was about her a new element, a kind of wistfulness, that the Dame, who had known Diana since before her marriage, had never detected before. Gently, she began to explore.

'What's the news from Rockport?' she asked breezily. 'Has any progress been made in retrieving the Rockport rubies?'

'Sheila remains stubborn. I've been tipped the wink that the trustees are going to issue writs. It'll mean some fairly nasty press.'

'Rupert can't be happy about that prospect.'

'He's not,' Diana agreed. 'He's also a bit miffed that the trustees aren't consulting him, and that Colin has taken over the campaign against Sheila. Colin's main worry, he tells me, is that he doesn't have enough hard proof that the wretched Sheila is sitting on the rubies.'

'Maybe not for the rubies, but what about the emerald? As I told you at the time, I saw Sheila wearing it just after the memorial service for Jamey.'

'Yes, I remember: and I told Rupert. But he says you're not an expert witness.'

'Stuff and nonsense,' said the Dame firmly. 'I may not be an expert, but I am independent and I do enjoy some standing. If it helps, I'm perfectly prepared to give an affidavit to the effect that the ring I saw on Sheila's hand is the same as that which the dowager wore when Rockport was first opened to the public. The old lady was draped all over, encrusted in every sparkler she could dig out from the vaults: and she told me specifically that the ring was an heirloom. And although I'm no expert in precious stones, I'd recognise that setting anywhere.'

'That's marvellous, Dame E., and Colin will be delighted.'

The Dame got up to fetch the coffee-pot.

'Mind you,' she went on as she refilled their cups, 'I'm

not convinced that resorting to the strong arm of the law is the best tactic with Sheila. The law is a blunt instrument; and apart from the disagreeable necessity to wash one's family linen in public, one can never be certain of the result.' She sat down again opposite Diana. 'It so happens that I'm dining at Lordstanding next week – a return bridge match. I might just take the opportunity for a few words with Sheila. Somebody's got to try and make her see sense.'

'I wish you luck. Rupert's tried much the same line: he's been hoping to get at Sheila through Betty Bassano, hoping that Betty might have some influence over her houe-guest.'

'But he doesn't seem to have made much progress?'

'He hasn't.' Diana was overcome by a sudden wave of desolation: even the Dame, old friend and ally, was consorting with Lordstanding. 'I didn't know,' she said, an acrid note of bitterness in her voice, 'that you too were on such good terms with Mrs Bassano.'

'My dear girl, come off it,' said the Dame with great good humour. 'Betty Bassano has made a good impression all over the county. Anyway, you've entertained her yourself at Rockport.'

'News travels fast,' said Diana, more lightly. 'I thought it would look rather odd if Rockport was the only house where she wasn't received.'

Betty's name, now raised, lay between them, almost a physical presence, like a large stone on the coffee-table.

'My dear, that was very brave of you,' said the Dame slowly, 'all things considered.'

'All things?' Diana repeated. Dame Elizabeth had edged open the door of her reticence: now she had to decide if she wanted to tear it down.

'I take it you know what's going on?' Diana's dark eyes wre levelled at the Dame, her pointed chin raised as if to take whatever blow was to come.

'I have a rough idea,' the Dame admitted cheerfully.

'I do hear things, you know.'

'Yes, I suppose it was too much to hope that there would be no talk.'

'People always gossip,' Dame Elizabeth pointed out. 'They can't help it, and you mustn't let if affect you or your actions.'

'But I'm not taking any action, and I shan't as long as I can avoid it. There's one thing that I'm terrified about; and that's that Rupert should find out that I know what's going on' — she took a gulp before adding — 'that I know about his affair with Betty.'

'And why is that, my dear?' prompted the Dame.

'Once Rupert knows I know, then the whole mess has come out into the open. Oh, I'd dearly love to have it out with him, indulge in a blazing row; but it wouldn't do any good — except perhaps to relieve my feelings. And once his attachment to Betty becomes an acknowledged thing between us, then he would be forced to make a choice. And I'm scared to death that if it came to that, he wouldn't choose me.'

'He will if he knows what's good for him,' said Dame Elizabeth grimly. 'That young man needs a good shaking to bring him to his senses. I remember his grandmother telling me that all the Jordans men were weak — that they need a determined woman to keep them on the straight and narrow.'

'Betty's no wimp,' Diana pointed out. 'She's attractive and charming and she's loaded. She captivates everyone she meets. Even I can see that she would make Rupert an excellent second wife.'

'Diana, you mustn't talk like that.'

'Why not? It's true. And that's what makes it worse for me. If Betty was a scheming vamp, then I could fight her like a tigress. But she's not: she's a delightful person whom I could well like if it wasn't for what she stands for.'

'You're too fair-minded by half,' said the Dame,

smiling. 'But I do see now why you've decided on a policy of ignorance. It's tough for you; but I agree it will be best in the end.'

'It's not only tough, it's lonely,' said Diana. 'I sometimes think I haven't an ally in the world, especially while Betty goes around conquering all. Thank God I've you to talk to, dear Dame E.'

'Not only me,' the Dame pointed out. 'You mustn't forget your mother-in-law.'

'Lorna? Yes, I think you're right, she was pretty icy to Betty after dinner the other night.'

'That'll have to change,' the Dame muttered, now deep in thought. Then she roused herself and said she was looking forward to having a frank talk to Sheila about the rubies.

'It would be wonderful if you could get them back for Rupert,' Diana told her. 'He really cares about his research and he wants to tie up this Carracci business before summer.'

There was an indulgence in Diana's voice that told the Dame what hadn't been voiced in their talk; that she still adored her husband and, like a mother with a beloved child, desired of all things to give him what he wanted. But the Dame had other things on her mind now, plans were formulating and she was itching to get to work on the telephone. Almost peremptorily, she bustled Diana into her coat and headscarf and out to the car.

Diana drove home in a much happier frame of mind. It had been good to talk to her old friend, to unburden her fretful thoughts; and it was a reassurance to know that the wily old bird was going to do battle with Sheila. If anyone could retrieve the return of Rupert's rubies, that person was, she knew, Dame Elizabeth de Blete.

Fourteen

The bridge party at Lordstanding was arranged for a Monday evening. The preceding weekend had been, for Betty, a trying time. Sheila's son, the wayward baronet Sir Joshua Fiske, had turned up, uninvited by either his mother or her hostess: for Betty, his charm was by now as threadbare as his cavalry twills, his presumption as disagreeable as his scuffed suede shoes. Sir Joshua retained a number of acquaintances from the days when he himself had lived in Mallamshire, and with these he filled the house from Saturday morning to Sunday evening, all of them eating copiously, drinking Betty's drink and running her Portuguese couple off their feet.

Through all the junketing, Sheila remained unruffled, smiling serenely. She remembered many of Joshua's friends and they clustered about her, flattering and teasing and at the same time showing their gratification that they were on such easy terms with the duchess. The girls Betty could not tell apart: they were all large, young and bouncy with loud voices and names like Fenella, Emily and Priscilla, and they shrieked. Goodness how they shrieked: on the tennis court, across the dinner table, up and down the stairs, at the backgammon board, they seemed incapable of anything less than a hearty bellow. As for the men, they were all a little older: Betty, with her American background, made an effort to catch their names: one was called

Hobhouse-Rees, he was almost portly, and said to be something in property, though an aside from Joshua suggested he had acquired a wealthy (and absent) wife along the road; and another, a raddled blond complacent of his looks, turned out to be the son of Mrs Hannah Cross whose chain-store business was famous for its enterprise.

It was a side of Mallamshire life that Betty had not until now encountered; and by Sunday night, she wasn't sure she wanted to again. On Monday, she told herself, the time had come for some plain speaking to her well-entrenched house-guest. But all day Sheila, perhaps sensing Betty's thoughts, kept out of her way and it wasn't until the evening, when they gathered in the library to await the arrival of Dame Elizabeth and Lady Alice, that Betty found an opportunity to speak her mind. There was at least half an hour before the bridge party, she saw after a glance at her clock.

Sheila, in a jersey wool dress with a large sapphire brooch on the lapel, was busy making herself a whisky and soda.

'Wasn't the weekend jolly?' she said brightly over her shoulder as she tinkled with the ice. 'I must say it does one good at our age to have the company of the young.'

Betty, who was an exact contemporary of Sir Joshua, did not take kindly to thus being bracketed with the older generation, and there was a crispness in her voice as she suggested that Sheila should come and sit down. 'It's high time we had a serious chat,' she said firmly.

'A serious chat? Oh good,' said Sheila, nestling in her usual corner of the sofa. 'I'm sure it'll do you good to talk about dear Rupert, and you know you can confide in me.'

'It's not about Rupert: it's about you. I think it's time you made some plans for the future. Of course, I've been happy to have you here at Lordstanding; but really you can't stay here for ever.'

'I hope I haven't outstayed my welcome?' Sheila sat up, her eyes narrow and wary.

'My dear Sheila, I'm thinking about you. You've been here for over six months now. For your own sake, you must look to the future, make up your mind where you intend to live, get on with your own life.'

'But you know perfectly well that I can't make any decisions until I settle things with the Jordans trustees. They haven't yet told me how they intend to provide for me, what income I shall have, where I can live.'

'Have you asked them? Has your lawyer?' Betty pressed.

'Mr Brash advises me to wait until we've settled this nasty business over my jewellery.'

'I see. Well, I've told you before, I think you're quite wrong to hang on to the heirlooms. Rupert needs the Rockport rubies, and it's horrid of you to sit on them.'

'I've said, time and time again, that I don't know about the rubies. I do know what my darling Jamey gave me, and nothing I've heard will persuade me to yield up the few precious things that remind me of our love. Why should I?' she wailed. A tear formed at the corner of her eye and trickled down her enamelled cheek.

'Because they are not yours, that's why,' said Betty unmoved.

Now the tears flowed freely. 'You don't know what it's like to be all alone in the world,' Sheila sobbed, 'and now even you have turned against me! I suppose you're going to throw me out of your house?'

'Don't be so melodramatic, Sheila.' Betty, exasperated, rose and went to look out of the window. The evening sunshine was slanting across the smooth green lawns: in the river valley below, by the blue-shadowed willows, it was already almost dark. Betty found herself remembering the many kindnesses shown her by Sheila and Jamey when she herself had been truly alone. Jamey Jordans had been a good friend when that was what she most needed; she could not now bring herself to be tough with his widow. She turned back and smiled down at Sheila, whose white hair was fluffed and dishevelled, her cheeks smeared with running mascara.

'You mustn't think I've turned against you,' she said gently, 'and of course I'm not going to evict you from Lordstanding. I'm only saying that you must give some thought to the future. And now,' she added briskly, 'you'd better run upstairs to your room and effect some repairs on your face before our guests arrive.'

Left alone, Betty felt frustrated that no conclusion had been reached. Perhaps the answer was for Betty herself to take a trip back to the United States, to close up Lordstanding and send the servants on vacation. For it was clear that nothing less than direct action would serve to dislodge the squatting Sheila.

When her guests arrived, Sheila also returned, her face restored, and Betty led them all into her card-room, a chamber hung with eighteenth-century Chinese wall-paper. It was done up as a gaming parlour, with tables for chess and backgammon as well as the green baize that was to be the arena for the evening's match. The bridge itself started slowly, with humdrum cards; and since Sheila, lips pursed and colour high, was still in a huff, the conversation was sporadic. They were dealing the third hand when Pedro came in and hovered beside Betty.

'Excuse, please,' he said, 'telephone for you, Señora.'

'Who is it, Pedro?' Betty was arranging her hand. 'Take a message, will you – say I'm busy.'

Pedro stood his ground. 'Is Duquesa,' he explained. He shot a black look at Sheila, who was not his favourite lady. 'Other Duquesa,' he explained.

'Diana?' Betty seemed uneasy. 'I wonder what she wants.'

She left to take the call in the hall; the others, intrigued, could not hear what was being said.

When Betty returned, she was smiling broadly. 'It

wasn't Diana after all,' she told them, 'it was Rupert's mother.'

'Lorna?' Sheila's delicate eyebrows were arched in surprise. 'What on earth did she want?'

'Lorna has asked me to luncheon at the Dower House.'

Dame Elizabeth permitted herself a half-smile: so Lorna Jordans had taken up her suggestion.

'I must say I was a bit taken aback,' Betty was saying. 'Lorna was decidedly frosty towards me at Diana's dinner party.'

'Well, I hope you haven't accepted,' Sheila snapped.

'Of course I have.'

'My dear, I'm not sure that was altogether wise.' From the way in which Sheila pursed her lips and began to arrange her cards, it was obvious that she resented the thought that her friend, her protegée as she liked to think of Betty, was proposing to consort with her predecessor; but she was constrained by the presence of the Dame and Lady Alice. Instead, she remarked with a sniff that really poor Lorna counted for nothing nowadays, and as for the way she continued to be addressed as 'Your Grace', why, everyone knew that a *divorced* duchess was not entitled to such a prefix.

It was during dinner that Lady Alice dropped her bombshell. She had been primed by the Dame during their drive over to Lordstanding, and she prepared the ground by admiring Sheila's sapphire brooch.

'I don't think I've seen it before,' she remarked.

'You probably haven't.' Sheila stroked the gems complacently. 'It was a present from Jamey last year, to celebrate our tenth wedding anniversary.'

'How generous my brother was,' Lady Alice said drily. 'And, talking of such things, I haven't seen you wearing my Mama's emerald recently. Do you have it with you?'

'I … I don't know. One has so many bits and bobs, I don't count them every day.' She gave a deprecating, tinkling laugh.

'I've seen you wear it, Sheila.' It was the Dame's voice, very firm indeed.

'Have you, dear coz? How observant of you. I didn't know you were knowledgeable about jewellery.'

'It was the day of the memorial service for your late husband.' Dame Elizabeth spoke with absolute authority. 'The ring was on your hand then.'

Sheila was beginning to feel cornered. 'I may have worn it then, but I don't remember. And I rather think I sent it back to the vaults in Nassau.'

'Its present whereabouts are irrelevant,' the Dame told her. 'What does matter is that you had the ring in your possession at a date after the death of your husband.'

'What is all this?' Sheila protested, looking round the table. 'I must say, I don't like your tone at all, Dame Elizabeth. I am not accustomed to being addressed as if I were a public enquiry.'

'Come off it, dear cousin.' The Dame seized the chance to throw back at Sheila the tiresome and tenuous relationship she made so much of.

'No, Dame Elizabeth, I see I must speak my mind.' Sheila rearranged her angora stole as if it was her dignity. 'My jewels are my business: certainly they don't concern anyone around this table.'

'Ah, but that's where you're wrong,' the Dame rejoined. 'And you'll do well to listen. The fact is that I have been approached by the Jordans trustees, and I have agreed to provide an affidavit in terms that I have witnessed you wearing an emerald ring that I know from the dowager duchess to have been a possession of the Duchess of Jordans 1920 Heirlooms Settlement.'

'So what?' The little duchess's cheeks were turning pink with rage, but she kept control of her voice as she added, 'Of course, I have intended all along to hand back that ring when I can lay my hands on it.'

'Don't you see, Sheila, whatever your intentions may

have been, the game is up. Now the trustees have proof that you have been retaining the ring, after several invitations to return it, they have every chance of persuading a court that the presumption must be that you are hanging on to the Rockport rubies as well. Your own lawyer will confirm that.'

The dam on Sheila's self-restraint burst. 'Blast you, Dame Elizabeth!' she cried. 'I'll see everyone suffers for your interference. Once the case comes to court, I'll spill the beans to every paper in the country. Your precious Rupert,' she added, turning to Betty, 'won't know what's hit him when I've called a press conference. There's nothing a columnist likes more than dirt in high places.'

'Sheila, you can't do that!' Betty's jaw had dropped, her face horrified.

'It would be most unwise,' Lady Alice agreed, giving her sister-in-law a hard look. 'I know I've been in the papers myself from time to time, but I've always done my best to keep the family out of it. You see, Sheila, in a family like ours, the one thing we avoid is washing our filthy linen in public.'

'I don't care,' said Sheila flatly. 'I've got to defend myself, with whatever weapon is to hand.'

There was a silence; then Dame Elizabeth spoke.

'Sheila is right, in a way,' she stated.

'Dear coz, I knew you'd understand.' Now the duchess was all smiles; with the Dame on her side, she had victory in sight.

'I meant,' the Dame went on, 'that you were right when you said that journalists have an appetite for dirt. So you will all be interested to know that this morning I had a long talk with my old friend Mr William Miller.'

Both Sheila and Betty looked blank: the name, so portentously announced, meant nothing to them.

'He's the editor of *The Mallamshire Gazette*,' Lady Alice explained.

'Oh, the local rag,' said Sheila dismissively.

'The *Gazette* is much respected in the county.' Dame Elizabeth sounded as if she was giving a reference. 'And Mr Miller is held in high regard by his colleagues in London. When he runs a story that is of more than local interest, he arranges that it is also carried by one of the national newspapers.'

'Get on with it, Dame E.,' urged Lady Alice. 'We're all longing to hear what you've been up to.'

'I gave him an exclusive. I retailed to him the facts as I see them. And a damned good piece he's woven out of them, if I do say it myself. He read it back to me this afternoon.'

'I wonder if, just this once, you may have been a little unwise, Dame E.?' Lady Alice was worried. 'I mean, a story in the *Gazette* is just what we don't need.'

'You wait until you see the story,' Dame Elizabeth chuckled. 'I'm afraid Mr Miller may have been a little hard on Sheila, but that's journalism for you.'

Sheila gave a little hissing noise. 'What do you mean, hard on me?'

The Dame waved her hand airily, clattering the bracelets on her arm.

'Oh, the usual heavily angled stuff – grasping stepmother, greedy widow, all that. And he's done rather well with the Rockport rubies: there's a stirring paragraph at the end that these heirlooms, now being held for ransom in a far-off foreign land, properly belong not just to the dukes of Jordans but to Mallamshire and indeed to England. These great historic relics, he declares, must be returned to their proper place in the bosom of our beloved county.'

This time the silence was prolonged.

'I think, Sheila, you've been pre-empted.' Betty spoke quietly.

'Of course I haven't. That rag would never dare to publish. And if it did, I'd sue.'

'You could; but actions for libel are always dodgy, and

anyway, for your purposes it would be too late. Mr Miller's story will certainly feature in the *Daily Mail*; and after that, even if you did call a press conference, nobody would believe what you said. They'd put your version down to sour grapes; and once journalists have taken a certain line, generally they don't bother to change it. Besides, my version does have truth on its side, and it's not malicious gossip.'

Dame Elizabeth made her points in a calm and reasonable tone, and this seemed to enrage Sheila.

'Malicious!' she shouted, 'of course it's malicious. My reputation will be ruined – I'll be a laughing-stock.'

Once again, she began to sob, the tears forming glistening runnels like snail-trails on her enamelled cheeks. Betty and Lady Alice, facing each other across the wreck of the table – crumpled napkins, half-empty wine glasses, crumpled bread and a spillage of salt beside a cellar – were half embarrassed and yet totally engrossed in the clash between the stalwart Dame and the diminutive duchess. Dinner itself was forgotten, as was the impending bridge game.

As, absently, she straightened a spoon, Betty was reminding herself that Sheila was her friend and, more important, her house guest. She needed defending against disaster.

She spoke up. 'I do think, Dame Elizabeth, that you are being extremely hard on poor Sheila.'

'No harder than she was prepared to be on Rupert – and, I would add, on you.' The Dame remained good-humoured, almost genial.

'Is there nothing you can do to stop that story being printed?' Betty was ignoring the implications of the Dame's remark.

'It is not for me to put a stopper on the great British press. But Sheila herself can do that, if she so desires.'

Sheila lifted her head, her beady eyes looking out through the fingers that covered her now raddled face.

'I can? How?'

Dame Elizabeth put her elbows on the table and began to explain.

'The *Gazette* goes to press tomorrow. Mr Miller is, to use his own phrase, holding the front page until he hears from me. If I confirm the story tomorrow morning, then he goes ahead and Sheila will be all over the nationals on Wednesday. But if I should tell him that I have now investigated further and I find that after all I have been misinformed, then the story will be spiked. That means it's killed off.'

'Then that is what you must do.' Betty spoke very firmly indeed. 'It would be cruelly wicked to let him print.'

'I will tell him just that – when and if I am satisfied it is true.'

Sheila reached out and laid her hand on the Dame's wrist.

'Dear coz,' she whispered, 'kill the story, I beg you, before it's too late.'

Dame Elizabeth detached herself from the other's grasp.

'As I've said already, the remedy lies in your own hands, Sheila. If I am to persuade Mr Miller to refrain from publishing, then I have to admit that I was wrong – that I have now learnt that the heirlooms are even now in the process of being returned to England.'

'I don't see the problem,' Betty put in. 'After all, you gave him the story in the first place.'

Dame Elizabeth gave Betty a gimlet glare, a look that had in the past served to silence a Secretary of State who spoke out of turn.

'The problem is that I have to know that what I say is true.'

'That's easy,' Betty persisted. 'I'm sure Sheila will give her word to make arrangements for the return of the rubies.'

The duchess, her face still hidden, nodded; but the Dame was still not satisfied.

'I fear that will not suffice,' she said grimly. 'I am minded to tidy up this whole unfortunate issue tonight.' She reached down into her capacious handbag, shuffled among its contents and pulled out three sheets of paper. 'In the hope that Sheila would be prepared to change her mind, I took the liberty of drafting some letters for her signature.

'The first,' she explained, 'is addressed to Mr Dunhill, the senior trustee at the Jordans office. In it, Sheila states that she has at last succeeded in locating the missing heirlooms and has now given instructions for their return to the trustees. Appended,' the Dame added, turning the page, 'is a list of the missing items, as supplied to me by Lord Colin.

'The second letter,' she continued, 'is to Sheila's lawyer, Mr Brash, and in it she informs him of her action and instructs him to withdraw her answer to the legal proceedings. And the third just gives the necessary orders to Sheila's bank. I am afraid I've had to leave their name and address blank. You will have to fill that in yourself, Sheila.'

Dame Elizabeth cleared a space on the cluttered table between herself and the duchess and laid down the papers. Betty was silent, stunned by the transformation of the jovial Dame into a formidable and remorseless woman of business; while even Lady Alice, who knew the Dame well, had nothing to say. They both waited, looking at Sheila for her reaction.

The duchess herself was hunched and quite still. Her hands still covered her face, like shutters closed across a window; but behind them, her mind was working furiously. By signing, she would be throwing away the prospect of extracting from the trustees what her lawyer had suggested might be a substantial sum of capital; but if she didn't do what the Dame wanted, then she would be pilloried and ridiculed not only in Mallamshire but in London and even among her circle on the other side of the Atlantic. Sheila put a high value on her rank and standing: it gave her a special status: and she knew as well as anyone how quickly and how permanently status could be tarnished. But first, she had a question. She put her hands on the table and looked straight ahead.

'If I sign your damned letters,' she said, 'I will be giving up the only weapon I possess in my fight to secure my future. Can you really be asking me to do that?'

The Dame nodded. 'I thought you might worry about that, so I had a word with Lord Colin. His view is that the trustees will be so relieved to retrieve the heirlooms that they won't hold the delay against you. They realise they will be expected to make provision for Jamey's widow; and it'll be up to your Mr Brash to negotiate the details.'

Sheila Jordans heaved a deep sigh. 'In that case, I'll sign. I don't have any choice, do I?'

'You don't,' said the Dame genially; and handed her a pen.

When the signing was done, the Dame took up the papers and looked around.

'Since we have here Mrs Bassano, Sheila's friend, and Lady Alice, her sister-in-law and a senior member of the family concerned, perhaps it would be as well if they signed too, as witnesses. That'll make it all watertight.'

Dame Elizabeth watched with satisfaction as pen and papers were passed around: then she gathered them up and stuffed them back into her bag.

'Well done, Sheila,' she said with the air of a headmistress congratulating a sulky fifth-former.

'Don't patronise me, you old cow,' said the duchess. She stood up, glaring down at the Dame's sparse grey hair scraped back into its usual bun. 'You've done nothing less than blackmail me. And as for you two –'

she looked from Lady Alice to Betty – 'you've both stood by and let this old bag ruin my future, so you'll understand that I'm not in the mood for a cosy rubber of bridge.'

The dining-room door slammed shut, and the three women remaining look from one to the other.

'Speaking for myself, I'm not too sorry about the bridge,' said Lady Alice, attempting a quiet and reasonable tone, 'but it's sad that Sheila can't see that thanks to Dame E., she's doing the right thing.'

'What we all need now,' said Betty, 'is a large, stiff drink.'

They adjourned to the drinks tray in the library, passing the gaming-room with its bridge table, cards, scorers and pencils waiting in mute reproach at the lost match.

When they were all settled, the Dame nursing a very dark Scotch, Lady Alice gave her a thoughtful look.

'Tell me, Dame E., were you really prepared to let the *Gazette* publish?'

'Oh, yes. For one thing, it doesn't do to issue a threat you are not prepared to carry out. And anyway, if Sheila was going to use the press herself, it was much better that the true version was made public first.'

'I still think you were bloody hard on poor Sheila,' said Betty, determined to stick up for her friend. Her manner was stiff: she hadn't expected total war to break out over her dinner table.

'Don't be too sorry for her,' advised the Dame comfortably. 'Underneath her dainty sweetness, she's tough and stubborn. Besides, she won't be a pauper, especially if the trustees advise her to maintain her overseas domicile and her tax-free status.'

'Do you mean that she'll go back to the Bahamas?' The hope in Betty's voice was so obvious that both Lady Alice and the Dame smiled, realising that Sheila had outstayed her welcome at Lordstanding.

'Not necessarily to Nassau: but I think she'll find it advantageous to live abroad. And there's one thing we three can do for her.'

Betty sat up, her wide face wary. The thought flashed through her mind that perhaps this bossy old girl was going to commandeer one of her houses in America for the duchess's use. But all the Dame was proposing was that they should all keep their silence about the events of the evening.

'We may as well let Sheila leave Mallamshire with her head held high,' she said. But she had another reason: the Dame had no intention of letting Betty be the first to give Rupert the good tidings that the rubies were on their way home.

Later, as she was driving Dame Elizabeth home to Braye, Lady Alice remarked that she had been impressed by Betty Bassano's loyalty to Sheila. 'It's quite clear she finds the wretched woman a pain in the neck, but that didn't stop her standing up for her guest.'

'Yes. The more I see of Betty, the more I like her,' the Dame agreed. 'That made my task more difficult.'

'Well, the whole Delaney-Grey family owes you a debt of thanks,' Lady Alice told her across the darkness.

'That's as may be,' returned the Dame gruffly. 'Anyway ...'

She didn't finish the sentence. But her friend knew what was in her mind. Dame Elizabeth liked human relationships to be orderly: above all things, she had a distaste for what she called untidiness, and the continuing affair between Alice's nephew Rupert and Betty Bassano was very untidy indeed. The Dame might have contrived the repatriation of the missing heirlooms: to arrange the return of Rupert's affections to their proper place would be very much more difficult.

Fifteen

On a bright day in May, Diana Rockport was driving over to Byegrove, her old home. The route took her over a wide plain, with vast fields bounded by stone walls where the broad horizon was only broken by the occasional skeleton of a dead elm tree; but her thoughts were not on the landscape: they were locked into the present whereabouts of her husband.

Dame Elizabeth had telephoned Rockport Place early on the morning following her démarche with Sheila Jordans. She had determined that Diana should be the first with the news, the first to tell Rupert that the rubies were on their way home. Diana had hurried back to the breakfast table, bringing the glad tidings to Rupert with the air of a spaniel laying a game bird at the feet of her master.

Rupert's response had been all that she could have wished. He leapt to his feel, his monkey-like face alight with glee. He had hugged Diana several times while the boys, catching his elation, began to scream with excitement until he hugged them too; then he had seized a second cup of coffee and hurried off to the business-room.

Later on, he had sought out Diana at her desk in the Dutch parlour. He seemed to have the impression that Diana had played some part in the retrieval of the heirlooms (which was just as the Dame had intended); at any rate, he thanked her thoroughly and went on to explain what he had been arranging. Appointments had been made for him to meet a representative of the security firm who looked after Rockport Place and a design specialist; this would take place at the estate office, when both experts would have the chance to take a look at the famous necklace.

'All absolutely secret, of course,' he told her. 'We want to keep the story under our hats until we can make a real splash when we open the display here. And with a newly-authenticated Carracci that shows the jewels as they were at the time of the Renaissance, I think we can be confident of hitting the headlines.'

Diana had enjoyed a renewal of confidence at Rupert's use of the plural pronoun; and they went on happily to a discussion of where best the necklace and the painting might be placed on show; Diana proposed a special display in the Great Hall, but Rupert suggested that that might be too soon on a visitor's tour of the house, that everything afterwards might be an anti-climax.

'I rather favour the staircase hall,' he said. 'We can place the painting on an easel where it gets the best natural light from the Venetian window above, and then put the necklace in a glass case beside it.' Then he frowned. 'Mind you,' he warned, 'I hope we're not being premature. We haven't had the rubies authenticated yet.'

'That's up to your Dutch expert, isn't it?'

'Yes.' Then Rupert had dropped his bombshell. 'The trouble is that the old boy is too frail to come to London. I'm going to have to see him again in Amsterdam, as soon as I can arrange for the jewels to be sent to a bank there.'

Amsterdam. The word thudded into her brain. It was only with an enormous effort of will that when she replied, she managed to keep her voice light, unconcerned. And this she contrived to maintain during all the fuss over Rupert's departure to London, his subsequent cheerful telephone calls to report progress and the one last brief chat from Heathrow before he flew off to Holland. There had been no suggestion that Diana might accompany him, and she wasn't going to suggest herself.

Now, in the car on the way to Byegrove, she forced herself to face the fact that Betty was almost certainly in Amsterdam too. She had heard on the grapevine from a villager whose cousin was gardener at Lordstanding that 'that Mrs Basin has taken herself off to foreign parts', it being generally understood that while Her Grace Sheila was packing her bags, the atmosphere was none too pleasant.

It had been on Diana's mind for some time that she should pay a visit to her old home. The house was still kept warm, and two gardeners worked hard to keep the splendid gardens immaculate; but despite the cost of all this, which waste worried Diana, for she was by nature thrifty, no decision had yet been reached about the future of the house. Diana had been reluctant to raise it, for to do so might reveal Rupert's intentions; but she realised that such indecision could not go on for ever.

She turned through stone pillars on to the gravelled drive and before her spread the house, its arms wide open as if to welcome her. The robust walls were honey-coloured in the sunshine, with batteries of tall chimneys like bulwarks at either end; under their dripstones, the stone-mullioned windows glittered with reflected light. Dear Byegrove, she thought. It was here that she and Rupert had first made love, had first declared their love, long, long ago, before they were even engaged. Here, in a flat in the stable courtyard, they had made their first home and here, when they inherited the house itself, they had together enjoyed the tender intimacies of bringing their sons through the excitements and the scares of infancy. It was a lovely place and if (if ... if ... if) a rift did develop between her husband and herself, she might count herself fortunate to be able to return to Byegrove.

She drew up in the forecourt. There was no time for further speculation, for both gardeners were waiting for her. They were two weather-beaten ladies, dressed identically in anoraks, navy slacks and pork-pie hats. Their names were Miss Lawrie and Miss Buss: the former was, inevitably, known as Annie, and the latter liked to be called Bill.

Diana greeted them both, somewhat effusively, for she was conscious of the length of her absence and knew that gardeners, like most people, have need of an audience and, more than most, deserve it.

'How did your open day go?' she asked breezily. The Byegrove gardens, famed throughout Mallamshire, were opened to the public twice a year under the National Gardens Scheme, at the end of April for the spring display of bulbs and again in June, when the herbaceous borders and the old-fashioned roses were at their best.

'A huge crowd, we had,' said Miss Lawrie in a soft, breathy voice. Despite her slight appearance, she excelled at the really heavy work – double digging, relaying of paving-stones – while the more hefty Miss Buss was a dab hand at pruning, hedge-clipping, grafting and the delicate task of encouraging reluctant cuttings into growth.

'Ever such nice people, too,' Miss Lawrie continued, 'they took a great interest in all our doings.'

'Too nosey by half, if you ask me,' put in Miss Buss gruffly. 'They all wanted to know what's going to happen to the house, now you and His Grace have moved into Rockport.'

She gave Diana a meaningful look, which her friend intercepted.

'Now, Bill,' she said warningly, 'that's none of our

business.'

'I think it is very much our business. I have to speak my mind, Your Grace,' she explained to Diana, 'and the plain fact is that there's not much satisfaction for Lawrie and me here if there's not folk in the house to enjoy our work. Might as well be on the staff of Hyde Park otherwise.'

'I do understand,' said Diana quickly. The last thing she wanted was to lose the altogether estimable Miss Lawrie and Miss Buss. 'His Grace and I have been so busy at Rockport, we haven't had time to give much thought to the future of Byegrove. But what I can tell you both is that if we do decide to let it – and we won't be selling it, I assure you – your jobs are safe. We'd make them a condition of the lease.'

'That's fair enough, as far as it goes,' Miss Buss conceded, 'but I do wish you'd get a move on.'

'Perhaps you're right,' said Diana, more to herself than to the gardeners. Then she suggested a tour of the gardens.

All was impeccable. There might have been too much formality for Diana's taste in the serried ranks of scarlet Darwin tulips rising out of a mist of forget-me-not that were bedded out in the sunken garden, but the polyanthus walk under the nut trees was a spangled triumph, and under the windows of the house were, as there always had been, banks of wallflowers, brilliant against the stone. Their heavy, acrid scent took Diana's thoughts back to her first season at Byegrove, when she and Rupert had together bedded out the spindly biennials. Then they went to take a look at the area by the green-houses, where thousands of summer bedding-plants stood ready in the frames. The kitchen garden itself was almost empty, little more than an expanse of tilth.

'No point in growing veg when there's no one here to eat it,' Miss Buss observed.

Miss Lawrie intervened to suggest that perhaps Her Grace would like some coffee, and they picked their way across the cobbled yard to the flat that had been Diana's first married home and was now occupied by the gardeners.

'I suppose you could grow vegetables for the restaurant at Rockport,' Diana put forward. 'I could have a word with the manageress at Effie Grey's pantry if you like, for it seems a pity not to make use of the kitchen garden.'

'No way,' said Miss Buss bluntly. 'That's commercial; and Lawrie and I, we're not market gardeners.'

'Never mind, it was just a thought.' Diana was beginning to realise that if the future of Byegrove was not settled soon, she stood in grave danger that the gardeners might leave for a place where their considerable talents were more constantly appreciated. When Rupert came back, she would have to face up to a decision.

After coffee, Diana decided to take a look around the empty house. First, she thanked the gardening ladies for all they were doing to maintain the glories of Byegrove, and promised to let them know as soon as she and the duke had made up their minds. Meanwhile, she added, she herself would pay a visit during the next open day; and she would also bring friends over to see the place from time to time.

As, aimlessly, she mounted the stairs, Diana felt a twinge of guilt. She knew that back at Rockport, three coachloads of New Zealand ladies had arrived. It was a good booking, with the promise of more, and Diana was well aware that the appearance of the Duchess of Jordans, circulating gracefully among them as they enjoyed their buffet lunch, would set the seal on their enjoyment of their tour. She was good at such occasions; but these days, she found that she had to draw on her nerves to chat with strangers: and she could ill afford such nervous expenditure. Such reserves as she had, she needed for her own private battle: to maintain a calm, cool face to Rupert, a cheerful and indifferent face to friends and staff and a loving face to the children.

On the top floor, she found herself in the nurseries, empty and swept bare, with dust motes dancing in the slanted sunshine; but here there were too many memories, and she hurried back downstairs to the morning-room, the place where she and Rupert used to sit in the evenings and where she had had her desk. It was still half furnished, with curtains, carpets and the old humped and crumpled arm chairs. But most of their favourite books, paintings and objects had been removed to Rockport, their places empty reminders of what had been the heart of the house. There was one small picture remaining, above the telephone: it was, she remembered, an etching and she bent down to look more closely at it.

Stained and foxed, its engraver unknown, it showed a typical Dutch scene of a bridge over a canal, somewhere in Amsterdam.

Amsterdam. That word again. The place where Rupert now was – and probably Betty too. Suddenly, she realised that the time was upon her for the making of decisions, however grave, however painful, however final. No longer could she go along, feigning indifference or ignorance.

First, she had to establish for certain that Betty was with Rupert. That was easy: a simply phone call to Lordstanding (as she had done, inadvertently, when first she found out). The manservant was not trained to discretion. And if Sheila should answer, well, Diana could always put the phone down.

Slowly, she dialled the Lordstanding number.

'Hallo,' a voice drawled almost at once.

It was Betty herself. Diana's mind went blank. What on earth could she, should she, say?

'Hallo? Hallo?' The instrument spoke.

'Is that … is that Mrs Bassano?' asked Diana, playing for time. 'Its Diana Jordans here.'

'Diana!' Betty sounded very surprised indeed. 'Were you wanting a word with Sheila before she leaves?'

'No … in fact, I didn't know she was on her way.' Diana was about to ring off and collect her wits, but Betty chatted on.

'Yes, Sheila is finally going, and not a day too soon as far as I'm concerned.' At the other end, Betty laughed. 'Between you and me, she's been pretty hard to take since the old Dame sorted her out, and I've been making excuses not to be here until she does pack her bags. In fact, you're lucky to have caught me: I'm off again this evening.'

'Oh? Where to?'

'Just London.'

'Ah.' There was a short silence. An idea had come to Diana: now was her chance to put it into action. 'Actually, Betty, I'm ringing from Byegrove. It's where we used to live before we moved into Rockport.'

'Yes, I've heard of it,' said Betty, 'and everyone tells me it's a very lovely place.'

'The gardens are looking spectacular at the moment, and the thought crossed my mind that perhaps you might like to come over and look around.'

'Why I'd love to. When would you like me to come?'

'Why not now?' Diana spelt out directions, saying it was about twenty minutes' drive from Lordstanding, and then added, 'I look forward to seeing you. It's time we had a chat.'

'It could be you're right,' Betty agreed, and rang off.

Diana slowly replaced the receiver. Soon, in a few minutes, she would know. With Betty, she intended to put her cards on the table, to find out exactly where Betty stood, how deeply she was involved with Rupert. Betty was straightforward, honest, she wouldn't stoop to dissemble; and if her answers revealed what Diana most dreaded, that, yes, she and Rupert were in love, then Diana would learn where she stood.

And where was that? Why, here in Byegrove, of course. It was to this safe, welcoming house that Diana and her sons would withdraw. Her patience and her capacity for tolerance were spent; and, although in Rupert's eyes her attitude might be seen as bourgeois, middle-class, it couldn't be helped; for she needed to retain some shreds of her dignity. And, love Rupert as she did with all her heart, even now, she would not stand in his way if he really wanted to take Betty as his second duchess.

Sixteen

Diana had only a few minutes before Betty was due to arrive at Byegrove. There was no time for a rehearsal of what she had to say, no time for regret that what she had let herself in for might mark the end of her marriage. First, she suppressed a rising panic and set off to observe the rites of hospitality. Luckily, she had left behind a few bottles of wine in the cellar, so she went down and drew out a Muscadet, found some odd glasses and washed them, drew the cork and took it all into the morning-room. Then she took herself off to the mirror in the cloakroom, where she applied herself to her face: checking her lipstick and patting her sleek dark hair into place. War-paint, she thought, smiling grimly at her reflection; though she still hoped that the encounter would not turn out to be a battle.

As she passed the hall window, she saw the nose of Betty's white Mercedes turning into the gates; she went out to stand on the steps below the porch as Betty drew up and dismounted. Betty was wearing fawn slacks and a fawn cashmere sweater: her tawny hair tumbled about her shoulders, over which she had slung a scarlet cardigan that gave her an air of casual swagger.

As they approached each other, both women paused. Each was wondering if they were on embracing terms: and, catching the thought reflected in the other's eyes, they both laughed, which served to break the ice.

Diana, with a glance at the sky where clouds were now

gathering, suggested that they had better go round the garden before the weather changed; so, side by side, they set off on the tour.

Betty proved knowledgeable and appreciative of the beauties of the famous garden. She exclaimed at the drama of the laburnum tunnel, now coming into bloom with its yellow tassels hanging like stalactites all along the vaulting green roof; and when she wanted to know exactly how the limes forming a wall around an Italian fountain-head were pleached, Diana took her off to find the gardeners and the answer.

The gardeners were delighted to explain; and they bridled at Betty's unstinted praise of their efforts. They were impressed, too, that Diana had so promptly redeemed her pledge to bring some visitors to admire their work, and it was with some difficulty that Diana eventually managed to tear Betty away and lead her back to the house.

'I'm most impressed, my dear,' Betty said. 'It's a superb place. But it must cost you a fortune to keep up, with no one living here to enjoy it all.'

There was a question in Betty's voice, which Diana saw no reason not to answer.

'It's a matter of keeping a promise,' she said, 'and if you'll come into the morning-room and have a glass of white wine, I'll explain.'

While Betty curled up in a corner of the shabby sofa, Diana poured the wine: then she sat down on a stool in front of the empty, gaping grate and began her story.

'Years ago, Byegrove was the home of Rupert's great-aunt, a remarkable old girl by the name of Lady Euphemia Fox. She came here when she was first married, before the first war, in which her husband was killed. It was as a memorial to him that she laid out these gardens which, apart from hunting, became her lifelong passion.'

'Poor old thing,' said Betty. 'But I don't see why

you've taken on the obligation.'

'Aunt 'Phemie was always fond of Rupert: and she was very kind to us when first we became engaged. You see, Rupert was then only a younger son; and I was quite penniless. Rupert's mother did not approve of me at all, and we had no prospect of a home of our own until Aunt 'Phemie took us in and gave us the flat in the stable yard. She also told us that she intended to leave us Byegrove in her will: and she asked us to promise that we would do all we could to maintain the gardens.'

'That was one hell of an undertaking,' Betty observed, sipping her wine, 'especially for a young couple without the means to do it.'

'It was a bit scary,' Diana admitted. 'I had a plan to turn Byegrove into a country-house hotel, which I thought would enable us to maintain the place and make a reasonable living. Then, suddenly, everything changed: I became pregnant and at the same time Rupert's elder brother was killed out riding and Rupert became the Earl of Rockport, heir to the dukedom and with an income to match.'

'Happily ever after, eh?' Betty grinned.

'It never is, you know that. Anyway, it was the time when Rupert's father was planning to bolt with your friend Sheila, and we had to rally round Lorna while all the family business was rearranged.'

'I thought you told me that Lorna didn't take to you.'

'She changed her tune. That's one of her many good qualities: she recognises when she's made a mistake and admits it. I'm very fond of Lorna: she's a remarkable woman.'

'She is indeed.' Betty spoke with such a positive air that Diana looked up.

'Of course,' she said, 'you had lunch at the Dower House the other day. I suppose she's changed her mind about you too?'

'You could say that.' Betty wore a strange, secretive

smile that aroused Diana's curiosity. At the same time, she felt a wave of loneliness at the realisation that Rupert's mother, like almost everyone else, had come to accept Betty as part of the Mallamshire scene. But there was no time at the moment for her to dwell on this thought. Could Lorna, hitherto loyal and loving to Diana, have been assessing Betty in the light of a prospective daughter-in law?

Betty, meanwhile, had gone off at a tangent, chatting about Sheila's future plans.

'Her latest idea is to take a house in the South of France. It seems she can afford it, and I think she's had enough of Mallamshire.'

'Good riddance,' said Diana. 'I know she's Jamey's widow and I know we should be kind to her for that reason; but I've found that whenever Sheila comes on the scene, we have to watch out for turbulence.'

'Yes, I've learned that in the last few months. I've not been able to think of Lordstanding as my own home since she arrived: in fact, I'm beginning to think she's put some kind of a hex on the place.'

'Still,' Diana said, pursuing her train of thought, 'it's strange that Sheila should choose the South of France. Did you know that Rupert's grandmother, the old dowager, used to live there? She had a villa on Cap Ferrat, and I can't remember if the trustees sold it after she died. If they still own it, perhaps they've offered it to Sheila as part of a settlement.'

'Sheila said nothing out it. She gave me the impression she'd found a house off her own bat – but then, she wouldn't like to give the trustees credit for anything in her present mood.'

Betty broke off to give Diana a long, level stare.

'I have to hand it to you, Diana,' she said, admiration in her face. 'You do know it all, don't you? Who lived where, whose aunt married whom, how those precious trustees will react: you have the whole darned family at your fingertips.'

'Oh, well.' Diana made a disclaiming gesture with her hand. 'In a family like the Delaney-Greys, one has to learn it. And I wasn't born to it, as I'm sure you'll have been told.'

'All the more credit to you, my dear. And you do the gracious duchess bit beautifully, too – which is more than I could ever do.'

'Do you think you might have to?'

'Ah,' said Betty. Then there was a silence. Diana watched as Betty's long, scarlet fingertips curled round the stem of her wine glass. 'I see,' she said very quietly, 'so that's what you meant when you said it was time we had a talk.'

On the stool, Diana sat up straight.

'I take it,' she began, her tone as dispassionate as a company secretary's, 'I take it you know that I am aware of what has been going on.'

'That I've been having a fling with Rupert? Oh yes. I think I knew you'd cottoned when we met in your bedroom after that dinner party at Rockport. I saw the knowledge in your eyes.'

'But Rupert doesn't know? You haven't told him?'

'He's still convinced you are blithely unaware. And I wouldn't dream of telling him – it's none of my business, and he doesn't like to talk about you to me. You know how he likes to keep the different parts of his life in separate compartments.'

Betty smiled, and Diana smiled back. They both sensed they were complicit in their understanding of the man between them.

'Mind you,' said Diana, 'I don't know how long we can keep him ignorant. I live in terror that some friend will blurt out that of course I've known about you and him for ages.'

'Surely not?' Betty looked worried. 'Rupert and I have always taken great trouble to cover our tracks.'

'You don't know Mallamshire very well. You can't keep a secret for long in the country, and I know for a fact that both Lorna and Dame Elizabeth are on to you, and as for Alice Brinscomb, she has the best nose in the county for a sexual indiscretion.'

'It's more than an indiscretion, Diana. It's serious.'

'How serious?'

'I don't know. You can't measure feelings with a ruler. But serious.'

Betty looked straight at Diana, whose dark eyes were hard and wide. 'You must think me a monster,' she said, her voice tinged with sadness.

'No, I don't,' Diana rapped out. 'At least, not really. Oh, I do admit that during the low hours of the night, I find myself hating what you represent – a threat to my family, my marriage, to all that Rupert and I have made together. But that feeling is something instinctive and certainly not personal. So, if you're a monster, it's an abstract monster.'

'What about jealousy – the green-eyed bit?'

'Jealousy is a horrible word, and it's nothing but destructive. Besides, if a woman really loves her husband, she shouldn't be surprised if another woman loves him in the same way; and it's a fact you and I have something important in common – and that's Rupert. But I do envy you,' Diana went on. 'I envy the time Rupert spends with you, the things he shares with you, and I have to face it that your compartment in his life is for ever an area from which I must be excluded.'

'I envy you, too,' Betty returned. 'I envy you that you are his wife, the mother of his sons, the central part of his world. You are the capital of his kingdom; I am only a distant province.'

'For the moment, maybe. But … you do want to have children of your own, don't you?'

'Yes, Diana, I do. More than anything in the world. And I'm thirty-nine – time is not on my side.'

Diana left the stool and went to stare out of the window. Outside, a storm had broken, bending a cherry tree in the wind: the spattering of rain on the window-panes sounded oddly loud.

'I'm not sure why we're having this talk,' Betty was saying from her place on the sofa. 'And if you're about to propose some kind of cosy pact – that you'll continue to be complacent provided I keep to my place as mistress – then I must tell you here and now it wouldn't work.'

'Of course it wouldn't.' Diana turned back to face the room. 'From my point of view, I've reached the end of the road as far as complacency is concerned. If you were just some bit on the side, I expect I could stand it. But you're not: you're attractive and warm-hearted and intelligent – just the sort of woman I'd expect my husband to fall for! I cannot share Rupert with you. And you'd like him to be the father of your children, wouldn't you?'

Diana moved away from the window to the shadowy corner where the Dutch etching hung. She felt that all the blood had drained away from her face, leaving it blanched, and she didn't want Betty to see. For, she felt as a cold clammy hand seized her heart, she had reached the end of the road. She had lost Rupert.

Betty rose up and came over to Diana's side. Gently she laid a hand on Diana's arm.

'If you had asked me that question a week or two ago, I would have had to give you the answer, yes. And we both know that if I worked on it, it is in my power to take Rupert away. For good.'

'Yes, we both know that,' Diana agreed.

'When we started our affair, I felt on top of the world. I was back home in England after twenty years, with the most delightful Englishman as my lover. There seems to be a natural progression in these things: from casual bed to full-blown affair, then a crisis, followed, often, by divorce and remarriage.'

'It often happens that way.'

'But need it, and should it? Whatever you may think of me, Diana, I am not by nature a home-breaker; and I have been beginning to realise that even if I swept Rupert off, I wouldn't necessarily have won him. You see, I know that his feelings for you and the boys are very, very deep.'

'Not deep enough, it seems.'

'Let's agree that he feels differently for you from the way he feels for me. After all, in his eyes, we occupy different pigeon-holes. And what frightens me is that yours will always be the most important to him, and that he would always look back with regret to what he had lost. I don't think I could bear to be second-best.'

'A lot of women wouldn't mind,' Diana said. It was strange, almost as if she were urging Betty to take Rupert, arguing the advantages. 'To be a duchess isn't to be sniffed at, even in this age of the common man. Quite apart from Rockport.'

'It's not enough for me,' Betty said firmly 'any more than it would be for you.'

'So what do you propose to do?'

'I … I don't know.' For the first time, Betty seemed hesitant, unsure of herself. She looked down into Diana's pale, heart-shaped face. 'A month ago, I would have been able to live with what I was doing to you. But now …'

'Why the doubts, Betty? Nothing's changed, has it?'

'I must be honest with you, and tell you that if I do now have doubts, they have nothing whatever to do with our talk here this morning. But I can say it is just possible that I may be making a mistake – I don't know for sure, but I owe it to you to tell you that at least.'

'I see.' For the first time, Diana permitted herself a tiny glow of hope. Betty, for all her tallness and her casual chic, seemed to have crumpled, to have lost her swagger. Diana suggested that they could both do with another drink, and they returned to their places by the tray, where Diana poured more wine.

'It really is rather strange,' Betty resumed in a more conversational tone, 'that you and I should be sitting here sipping wine and discussing our situation as if we were trying to choose a nanny. Without rancour, too – and we could easily have slipped into a slanging match. But, speaking for myself, I've no hard feelings.'

'Nor have I,' said Diana.

'In fact, I remember that evening when we met in your bedroom, I had then the oddest feeling that one day we might be friends.'

'I felt just the same,' Diana agreed. 'I longed to talk properly to you, even then.'

Betty put down her glass, with the air of one coming to a decision.

'Look Diana,' she said, 'I can't make you any promises. I'm in a muddle and I need time to think. You know I'm on my way to London?'

'Yes, you said you wanted to escape from Sheila's tantrums.'

'Well, I think I'll stay there. I'll take a service flat and go to ground for, say, a month. And I'll give you my word that during that month I won't see Rupert or even tell him where I am.'

'You will have to tell him something – you can't just disappear. He might be rather hurt.'

'I'll write to him; but don't worry – I'll let him down lightly.'

She smiled: and Diana thought how odd it was that the two women in Rupert's life were taking such elaborate care of his feelings.

'He mustn't know that we've been talking together, either,' she went on. 'He'd be dreadfully unnerved if he found out that we'd been putting our heads together.'

'I agree: it's our secret. Meanwhile, I'll try to sort out my future plans while I'm in London: and as soon as I come back and whatever may happen, we must meet again.'

Betty now rose to her feet and announced she must be on her way. They went together out on to the forecourt and this time there was no hesitation: they embraced and Betty drove away.

Seventeen

When Rupert Jordans returned from Amsterdam, he was jubilant. He burst into the Dutch parlour, where Diana was at her desk, embraced her with exuberance and at once embarked on a narrative of his success with the Dutch professor.

'The old boy quivered with joy when he got his hands on the rubies,' he told her. 'He felt them and stroked them and even held them against his cheek; and when, finally, he took them to his lab, he was able to confirm without doubt that the stones are of the finest quality and that the settings are Italian work of the *cinquecento*. It is, he says, the finest Renaissance piece he's ever set eyes on, and the workmanship is superb. In fact, he looked like bursting into tears when finally he had to put them back in their box.'

'Rupert, that's wonderful,' said Diana, catching his excitement, 'and it's a triumph for all your work and scholarship that you've proved their provenance. Well done, my darling!'

As, impulsively, she took his hand, she looked into his face. His dark eyes were dancing with triumph, his monkey-like features beaming and his fresh complexion flushed: he looked more like a school prefect who had won a major prize than a middle-aged duke whose marriage might be on the rocks.

Diana knew very well just how much it meant to him that all his hard work, his solitary hours spent poring over dusty ledgers in the archives, his checking of cross-references and his delving into the darker corners of his family's history, had now been vindicated; but, wife-like, she felt she had to add a note of caution.

'The rubies must be tremendously valuable now,' she pointed out. 'Will it be safe for us to display them here?'

'That's up to the security people,' he said. 'They seem confident they can fix us up with a bag of tricks that will foil most thieves.'

'Then we have to decide where to show them. And I've been thinking that you're right: the staircase hall will be the best place.'

'The Carracci is due back from the restorers in a fortnight. We can see then how it looks under the stairs. But,' he added excitedly, 'we have a tremendous amount of work to do before we're ready to show my discoveries to the public.'

'Press release, publicity plan, television preview, private viewing,' said Diana, ticking off the items off her fingers.

'All that,' Rupert agreed, 'and I can't wait to make a start. I think I'll trot along to the business-room now and get down to it all with Jean. Are you going to join us?'

Diana could see that he was raring to go; and she was deeply pleased that he suggested she join him, for in recent months he had shown a preference for working on his own; but she knew (for she had seen the envelope on his desk, though she did not know the contents) that Betty's letter was waiting for him. But she did not want to embarrass him – and perhaps force him to equivocate if not lie – by making him read the letter before her eyes, so she said she would finish her own work and join him later.

When she did go to the business-room, she found both Tom de Blete and Jean Wright gathered round Rupert's desk. Papers, notes and plans covered every surface, decisions taken, plans made, and the atmosphere, that of a team happily engrossed in absorbing and constructive work, reminded Diana of the old days, before Rupert's attention and energies had been diverted elsewhere.

'The Dutch professor is going to write a scholarly piece for *The Burlington*,' Rupert was saying, 'and I'm going to contribute an article for *Country Life*. That should start the publicity ball rolling.'

'In that case, we don't want to have the public launch until both journals have published,' Tom de Blete remarked. 'That means the end of June, at the earliest.'

'Half-way through our season,' said Jean, 'but it can't be helped.'

'And all our guides for the year are already printed,' Diana pointed out. 'We can't just scrap them – and yet we must say something about the painting and the rubies. Why don't we buy some off-prints of your article, Rupert? They'll serve until we can reprint the official guide.'

'Good thinking, darling.' He grinned at her while Jean was making another note: his round, nutlike face wrinkled up as he smiled and Diana felt again a warming hope that things between them might be on the mend.

Rupert said nothing about his letter from Betty until the evening, and when he did refer to it, it was only obliquely. They were having their before-dinner drink in the library: both had spent an indulgent time in the nursery with their boisterous sons and were in need of a whisky and soda. Rupert was busy with the decanter and he spoke over his shoulder.

'By the way, I'm afraid I'm going to have to make another trip to Lordstanding.'

For a second time, Diana felt herself freeze. Was the unhappy pattern beginning again, had Betty gone back on her word?

'There was a long letter from the trustees in my postbag,' he was continuing, 'and it explained all the arrangements they propose for Sheila. They want me to see her before she leaves England, just to make quite sure she knows exactly how she stands. And it would be a courtesy anyway, to bid her farewell. Besides, she must be a bit lonely: I gather Betty Bassano has taken herself off.'

Diana made no comment; but she was watching Rupert closely, though he didn't know it. She wanted to see if he was upset by Betty's removal of herself; but Rupert seemed no more than mildly curious.

A few days later, he returned from his mission to Lordstanding.

'How was Sheila?' asked Diana. It was again in the evening, and again Rupert was in need of his whisky. 'I must say, I do feel a bit sorry for the poor little woman. She must feel she has been hounded out of Mallamshire.'

'You needn't feel too sorry,' Rupert replied, flinging himself into a deep chair and easing his feet on to a stool, where they crumpled that week's *Spectator*. 'She's certainly not poor; and she didn't behave at all well. She's lucky the trustees decided to be generous.'

'Is it your grandmother's house on Cap Ferrat that she's going to live in?'

'No, that would need an army of servants to keep up. Luckily, it's just been sold to some bogus Swiss count, so we've a good number of French francs in the bank. The trustees have told Sheila they will buy her a villa of her choice – up to a limit, of course.'

'That's fair enough; but what will she live on?' Diana was surprised at her concern for Sheila's wellbeing, for her stepmother-in-law had been nothing but trouble since she arrived in Mallamshire, and she was pretty sure that Sheila had encouraged Betty to entangle with Rupert. Perhaps it was that she had a glimmer of fellow-feeling for the previous duke's widow.

'Sheila is not a pauper – she's inherited everything that my father had of his own to leave. But the trustees will provide her with additional income: they are setting up a trust fund in Geneva with the rest of the French francs. That will revert to the trustees when she dies – and so will the villa. Sheila didn't like that at all. I had to make it quite clear that the trustees felt no obligation whatever to the sons of her first marriage.'

'And she's handed back the rest of the heirlooms?'

'She tried to sit on Grandmama's emerald ring, but I finally persuaded her to hand it back this evening.' He reached into his pocket and took out a crumpled piece of tissue paper. 'And here it is.'

He tossed the package over to Diana, who fielded it neatly and unfolded the tissue. The ring lay in the palm of her hand, its great, square-cut stone flashing green.

'Go on, darling,' Rupert urged, 'put it on. It's yours now.'

Diana slipped it on to a finger and held it up to the light. The ring fitted perfectly.

'I've always wanted you to have it,' Rupert said quietly, 'and on your hand it looks absolutely lovely.'

'Maybe.' Then she slowly drew the ring off and laid it on the table beside her. 'But it's not mine.'

'What do you mean? Of course it's yours. From me to you.'

'That's not true, Rupert. That ring is not yours to give, nor mine to receive. In your dealings with Sheila, you and your precious trustees have made that quite clear. The ring is nothing more than an emblem of office – like a major's crown or a chauffeur's cap.'

They argued, without conclusion, for some minutes. Diana was hurt, more hurt than she cared or dared to show. It was painful that Rupert did not understand that she would love a present only if it was from him, chosen by him for her. To be tossed a bauble from his family's hoard was not the same thing at all. But none of

this could she express, so she closed the issue by
declaring that if Rupert so wished, she would flaunt the
emerald on suitable public occasions.

'But green is not my colour,' she added, with the air of
one making a final and conclusive point.

Rupert sighed and eased his legs off the stool before
going to refresh his glass. As he passed her, she saw that
his face wore a look of bafflement, as if he was mystified
by the workings of the female mind. In the old days, she
thought sadly, in the days before Betty, he would have
known intuitively, without a word being spoken, how
she felt.

But Rupert was changing the subject.

'There's a bit of a mystery at Lordstanding,' he was
saying. 'It seems that Betty has decamped, without a
word to anyone about where she's gone.'

'Yes, I'd heard something of the kind.' Diana
managed to sound off-hand. 'They say the atmosphere
at Lordstanding was rather fraught, with Sheila in a
terrible temper, so I expect Betty decided to leave. After
all, there's nothing to stop her, and she has lived in the
States for many years. You know what Americans are
like – they never stay in the same place for long.'

'I know all that,' Rupert persisted, 'but it does seem
odd. She hasn't even left a forwarding address – not
even the servants know where she is.'

Diana said nothing, but she smiled to herself. So Betty
had honoured her pledge, as Diana had known she
would.

During the following three weeks, Betty's name was
not mentioned between them. They were both
extremely busy: planning for the publicity drive, which
they hoped would double their gate for the rest of the
season, was often interrupted by the arrival of a
succession of experts from the art world, whose
self-important assumption that they were entitled to the
privilege of a private view of the new treasures of

Rockport Place took up much time. The experts also assumed that their presence demanded entertainment, usually a lunch. Diana, with a lengthening list of tasks to be completed before the end of June, was inclined to be irritated by the interruptions; but Rupert said they were well worth while, for word of mouth was the best publicity of all.

From time to time, Diana found herself wondering how Rupert was taking to the absence of Betty. On the surface, he was mildly cheerful, his self-possession undented; it seemed as if he didn't give Betty a thought. It was probable that in his compartmenting way, he had simply slammed shut the drawer in the bureau of his mind that was labelled 'Betty': would he open it again when once more she appeared on the Mallamshire scene?

Diana was surprised to find that the moral issue did not obtrude. In herself, she possessed a strong sense of what was right and wrong, and from her point of view, Betty's presence between them was not to be tolerated within her marriage. At the same time, she accepted that Rupert's own values, as might be expected from his background, were more cavalier: but no more would she stand for him to be cavalier to her. Occasionally, her courage wavered, as she wondered if it had been madness to trust her future to 'the other woman'; but generally she managed to keep her nerve, and Rupert sensed nothing different in his wife's manner.

It was in the second week of June, when Diana was feeling particularly confident about the future, that Rupert, with one sentence, shattered her peace of mind. They were, as so often that month, gathered in the business-room with Tom de Blete and Jean Wright: the task for the day was the guest-list for the private view, for which Rupert's mother Lorna had been conscripted to help, for she was skilled at the important part of such a list, those who would be offended by their omission.

'What about Betty Bassano?' Rupert put in, 'we really must ask her.'

'No point – she's away.' Diana's answer came out more crisply than she intended.

'She's back at Lordstanding,' Rupert answered. 'I spoke to her on the phone only an hour ago.'

Diana felt her head swim. She had been betrayed. For had not Betty promised that when she returned to Mallamshire, Diana would be the first person she saw? Yet here she was, back to the old routine.

Then, through the mists, she heard Lorna talking.

'I think that's a very good idea,' she was saying. 'Mrs Bassano is quite one of us nowadays.'

Lorna went on about Betty's qualities. In fact, she was the only one of the company who faced Diana, and she had seen the effect of Rupert's casual suggestion to his wife. She was only talking to fill in time, to give her daughter-in-law time to recover her poise. But Diana didn't know this: and she could only assume that Lorna, succumbing to Betty's charm and mesmerised by her prodigious wealth, had gone over to the other side.

She shot the elder duchess a hard look. To her amazement, Lorna made a quick, assuaging gesture with her left hand and then, on the side of her face turned away from Rupert, gave Diana a quick wink. Diana was mystified; but she had no time to find out what Lorna meant, and the gesture steadied her sufficiently to bring her back to the next item on the agenda, the provision of catering facilities for the voracious television crews that were expected to cover the unveiling of Rockport's latest discoveries.

Later, that evening while Rupert was in the bath, Betty Bassano rang again. This time, Diana took the call.

Eighteen

On the last morning in June, Diana Jordans came hurrying down the oak staircase at Rockport Place. She was wearing a simple linen skirt in gentian blue that swirled with each light step, and she was humming happily to herself. She passed through the great hall and emerged on to the perron which lay below the vast stone columns that formed the portico.

She breathed in the soft air. It was going to be a beautiful day; already the sun was dissolving the last wreaths of mist that lay over the blue surface of the lake. Beyond the dappled water stood the Greek temple, white in the slanting rays of the sun, and in the deer park the magnificent trees – beech, oak and cedar of Lebanon – rose above the rich green of the grazed grass, as artfully disposed as Lancelot Brown had intended when he supervised their planting, two hundred years ago.

Diana leaned against one of the columns, taking in the view. It was quite still; not a breath of wind, nor yet the raucous voices, the coaches, the cars and – worst of all – the kiddies of the daily visitors disturbed the tranquillity. At her back, she could feel the strength of the stone, already warm in the sun; and she realised, quite suddenly, that she had come to love the vast house that loomed behind her.

It was quite ridiculous, really: Rockport Place was more a palace than a home, a monument to the past dignities and the acquisitive greed of the dynasty into which she had married; but she knew now that for all its echoing corridors and its countless rooms, it was home: home to her, home to the boys now clamouring for their breakfast in the nurseries on the second floor, home to her husband, still tousled with sleep in their bedroom.

She turned back into the house; and as she passed through the staircase hall, she encountered Dobson, salver tucked under his arm, intent on some mystic butlerian errand.

'Good morning, Dobson,' she greeted him, 'isn't it a lovely day?'

She was amazed to think that once she had been frightened of this kindly old man.

'Good morning, Your Grace,' he returned, with a slight bow, 'and I trust that congratulations are in order? I have placed all the newspapers in the small dining-room, as you ordered.'

'Thank you Dobson,' she smiled, and went on down the corridor, her heels tapping on the stone flags while Dobson smiled affectionately at her sprightly retreating figure.

At the breakfast table, she fell on the stack of papers. They were all there and they had all done Rockport proud, after the press conference of the day before. *The Times* carried a large photograph on the front page, with the caption 'Major Heritage Discovery at Duke's Home': the *Telegraph* and the *Independent* both ran long, serious articles about the importance of the link between the Carracci and the rubies as a unique contribution to the history of art: while, at the bottom of the scale, the *Sun* proclaimed, in flaring headlines, 'Rupe the Duke scoops the Loot!'

At this last, Diana grinned: Rupert would be in for a good deal of teasing before the day was out. Still, they said that all publicity was good, and it looked likely that Rockport's takings at the gate that season would be considerably boosted. But her mind was not on the press coverage: she was looking for another item, and she picked up *The Times* and turned to the Court page.

There it was.

Lord Colin Delaney-Grey and Mrs E. Bassano

The marriage took place recently, quietly in London, between Lord Colin Delaney-Grey, younger son of the late Duke of Jordans and Lorna, Duchess of Jordans of The Dower House, Rockport, Mallamshire, and Mrs Elizabeth Anne Bassano, daughter of the late Major Denis Box, M.C., and the late Mrs Box, of Lordstanding, Mallamshire and Jackson Hole, Wyoming.

Diana read the announcement again and again. Now she saw it enshrined in print, she felt as if her ship had safely come home to port after a long and hazardous voyage. She poured herself a cup of coffee, and her mind went back to the day when she first heard the news.

When Betty had telephoned Diana, she had been brief, almost brusque. She said merely that she had to see Diana, and soon, suggesting that they met again at Byegrove. The next morning, Diana had taken the familiar road to her old home with her mind in a state of suspension: she would not jump to conclusions, she must wait to hear what Betty had to say.

Betty's car had already been parked outside Byegrove's porch and as Diana dismounted Betty came up to her, arms outstretched.

'Dearest Diana!' she cried, 'I have the best of all possible news!'

Diana was a little stunned by this; but Betty took her arm and together they entered the house.

'First, I owe you an apology,' Betty said, with a rueful moue. 'I didn't mean to talk to Rupert until I'd seen you; but when I gave my name to the girl who answered the phone at Rockport, she must have assumed I wanted to talk to him, not you. When he spoke, I couldn't think what to do, so I just told him I was back for a few days and I'd be in touch later.'

'I understand,' said Diana, relieved, 'and it was an easy mistake to happen.'

'And, talking of mistakes, when I think of what I nearly did ...' Betty broke off. 'Look, do you think we could sit down? I have a lot of explaining to do. Do you remember that when we last sat here, I said it was possible I was making a mistake? About Rupert, I meant.'

'I remember it well.' Diana had been over every word of that conversation in her mind during the intervening month.

'Then it was just an instinctive feeling. A sense that I had got things dreadfully wrong. And I've discovered I had: I was falling in love with the wrong brother!'

'What on earth do you mean?' Diana was mystified: she couldn't see how Colin came in to the picture.

'At first, I didn't really notice Colin at all,' Betty explained. 'Oh, he was nice enough as far as looks go, but he always seemed to hover in the background, overshadowed by his brother.'

'That happens,' said Diana, 'especially in families like ours.' She remembered the days when Rupert himself had been a younger brother.

'Colin came to my Christmas party; we met again at your dinner, and after that I saw him occasionally; but always in company, and always when Rupert was present, so I never paid him much attention. Until, that is, I went to lunch at the Dower House.'

'That was a bit of a shock to me,' Diana confessed. 'I had assumed that Lorna was on my side.'

'It was a surprise to me too. Rupert's mother had been positively glacial to me: and yet, when I arrived at her house, she turned out to be friendliness itself. I soon realised the reason for her change of manner; for we were only four to lunch, and the fourth was Colin.'

'A little too obviously contrived, don't you think? Didn't that put you off?'

'It didn't strike me that way. If I'd thought about it, I'd just have assumed that Lorna was taking some trouble to show me she had another son. But, by then and even over her luncheon table, Colin and I had struck fire.'

Diana looked at the other woman. Betty's wide face, with its generous mouth and warm brown eyes, seemed alight: she was iridescent with happiness and with fulfilment. Diana felt very glad indeed, as she always was when friends came into love: and below her pleasure there was welling up the most profound relief.

'So,' she said, smiling broadly, 'it was love at first sight?'

'I honestly think it was.' Betty sounded humble as she made the admission. 'We hit it off right from the start: and in the last month, while I've been in London, we've seen each other almost every day. Colin and I know we are made for each other.'

'And what happens now?' Diana was being told so much, and of such importance, that she could hardly take it all in.

'Can you stand the thought of having me as a sister-in-law? After all I've put you through, I wouldn't blame you if you never wanted to see me again.'

'Don't be ridiculous, Betty. I'm absolutely delighted, both for you and for Colin.'

'That's a relief. For what you feel matters to me. I wouldn't want you to see me as a hideous reminder of a beastly period in your life, every time I loomed up at a family gathering.'

'You needn't worry. I intend to put the whole episode behind me, and welcome you into the family with open arms.'

'You're a remarkable woman, Diana. But what about Rupert? How do you think he'll react?'

'Knowing Rupert as we both do ...' It was a tribute to the growing friendship between them that when Diana said this, they both burst into laughter.

'Knowing Rupert,' Diana eventually continued, 'I expect he'll just take you out of the pigeon-hole labelled "girlfriend" and pop you into a new one called "Colin's wife". But,' she added more seriously, 'you're the one who's going to have to tell him.'

'I know. And he deserves the truth – that I was and remain very fond of him, but that as far as the physical side was concerned, he was just the forerunner.'

'Don't be too hard on him, Betty. His pride will take a battering anyway, when he learns that he's been superseded by his young brother.'

Perhaps Diana was being over-protective of her wayward husband's feelings; evidently Betty thought so, for she replied quite sharply that after the hurt he'd inflicted on Diana, a little pain would do him no harm at all.

'Mind you, Diana,' she went on, 'I have no regrets, apart from putting you through the mill. He gave me a wonderful time, and he made my return to England very happy. To be honest, looking back I believe I was more in love with England, as represented by Rupert, than I ever was with him as a man.'

Diana understood why, now, Betty felt a need to depreciate Rupert: but she felt she had heard enough, so she asked if they had yet made any firm plans for the future.

'We're going to be married as soon as possible: just a Registrar's office in London, then a short trip abroad, to the Cipriani in Venice.'

'I hope you'll be back by the end of June.' Diana had an idea. 'You see, Rupert and I will be having a party then – a sort of private view for our friends to see the rubies and Rupert's painting – and it would be lovely if you two could be there. It would be a chance for you both to show yourselves to Mallamshire as Lord and Lady Colin.'

Betty saw the point and promised they would return in time.

'And there's another favour you could do us. Colin and I were wondering ...' There was a smile of rich inward pleasure on Betty's face as she paused, and Diana smiled back, knowing exactly the deep satisfaction felt at the phrase 'Colin and I'. It was a declaration of shared love, shared life, shared purpose.

'We were wondering if you might consider letting us live at Byegrove.'

'Here? Honestly, Betty, I thought you already had more homes than you know what to do with.'

'Yes, but none of them are right for Colin and me. We're determined to live in England; but Lordstanding won't do. In some way, Sheila tainted it, and I want to put the past few months behind me and start again with Colin somewhere new.'

'I did offer Byegrove to Colin ages ago, and he turned me down. What's made him change his mind?'

'It's rather sweet, really. You see, I'm by way of being almost indecently well off; and he wants to feel that he too is contributing to our future life together. By providing our family home, he would be doing just that.'

'I see that.' Diana was thinking hard. 'It's certainly an idea. Mind you, we couldn't offer you a lease of more than twenty-five years. At the back of my mind, I've always thought it might be good to have Byegrove available for Jonathan when he settles down and gets married.'

'My, you do plan far ahead!' Lord Jonathan couldn't be more than six years old. 'I think we'd be prepared to give way to Johnnie when the times comes.' Betty's tone was dry: she wasn't yet accustomed to the financial far-sightedness of families such as the one she was marrying into.

'And you'd have to promise to keep up the gardens,' Diana stipulated. 'That would mean cajoling Miss Lawrie and Miss Buss to stay on.'

'I'll have a talk to them before I leave.' Betty was intent on meeting Diana's every requirement: for above all things she wanted Colin to be enabled to bring to their marriage this warm and beautiful old house.

'In that case,' Diana decided, 'Byegrove is yours.'

She added that for form's sake, it would be best for Colin to apply to his brother for the lease, but they both knew that in fact the matter was already settled between the two women; and then Diana had to hurry away, leaving Betty to prowl, planning, through the empty rooms of the house that would soon be her married home.

At her own breakfast table and armed with a second cup of coffee, Diana smiled as she remembered how easily the arrangements had been agreed. Rupert had been very quiet for a day or two after his last private encounter with his brother's wife-to-be: he kept out of Diana's way, finding tasks that took him out and about the estate (much to the satisfaction of the agent, who had grounds for feeling neglected). Then, very gently, he had set himself to the delicate task of wooing his wife.

Diana had watched him with an inner amusement that she could never show, any more than she would reveal her knowledge of his affair. He was winning, affectionate, companionable; and the obvious pleasure he took in her company and that of the boys began to convince her that his feelings for her were indeed as deep and well-founded as hers for him.

Rupert had now himself arrived at the breakfast table and Diana stirred herself to provide him with his coffee.

But he didn't take his chair.

'The papers have done us proud,' she told him. 'We'll have to be ready for a record crowd of visitors this afternoon. And Colin's marriage is in *The Times*. So one way or another, it's quite a day for Rockport.'

She looked up to smile at him. He had not yet sat down, but continued to hover beside her, ignoring the spread of newsprint. He had just emerged, fresh from his bath, his cheeks still damp; and casually dressed, in jeans and a shirt open at the neck to reveal a tuft of black hair at his throat, he looked so like her old, boyish Rupert that her heart turned over.

'I ... er ... I've got something for you,' he said gruffly. He put before her a small tooled-leather box and turned away to stare unseeingly at the face of a bracket clock that ticked out the minutes on a console table set between the windows.

Diana opened the box. Resting on a cushion of dark velvet there lay a brooch. In the shape of a heart, with a glowing blue lozenge-shaped sapphire at its centre surrounded by diamonds, it was Victorian workmanship at its best: some might consider it sentimental, but Diana knew at once that it was precisely her taste, her style.

'Darling, it's perfect. And very beautiful.'

'After that fiasco over the emerald I wanted you to have something that really is from me to you.' Rupert was still facing the clock, his back to the table. 'It is to say thank you.'

Diana left her chair and moved over to his side.

'I really don't know what I've done to deserve such a present,' she said, keeping her voice light.

'I think we both know why,' he answered. 'We don't have to put it into words, but we both know.'

Diana looked straight at him. His olive-black eyes were very serious. So, after all those months, he knew: at last, he had realised that his wife had borne alone the hurtful knowledge of his affair, of his withdrawal of his affections from her.

She closed her eyes for a moment of sheer thankfulness. There would be no need now for any further dissembling on her part, no need to shield her inner thoughts from him, no need to maintain a cheerful, proud facade. Nothing had to be said: there would be no humiliating beggings for forgiveness on his part and no flaring expressions of injured pride on hers. They would emerge together from the dark times with their marriage enriched and more solid than ever.

She turned to him and he folded her into his arms. They stayed embraced for a few seconds, then Diana broke away with a laugh, saying he had better have his breakfast at once, for there wasn't much time before Colin and Betty were due: and then the party would begin.

By half past twelve, both the great saloon and the green drawing-room were full. The company – friends, neighbours, local dignitaries and those who could not be left out – formed an orderly queue to stare at the new treasures: the great Carracci, with the pink, fleshy form of Aphrodite recumbent as her plump fingers toyed with the jewels that were her tribute of love: and the same jewels, dazzling rich and red under spotlights behind the safety of a reinforced glass showcase.

Another centre of interest was, of course, Lord Colin and his new Lady. The announcement in *The Times* had been for many their first intimation that what they thought of as their exclusive knowledge of the duke's private life was, to say the least, inaccurate, especially when they saw on what affable terms the duchess was with her new sister-in-law. Among these were several who felt uneasy that their effusive acceptance of the newcomer Betty and, indeed, their often whispered speculation that she might become Rupert's second duchess, might have damaged their standing as regards

Rockport Place: these had been relieved to receive their invitations and now they made certain that Diana noticed them, clustering around her, clamorous in their expressions of friendship.

For this occasion, Diana and Rupert made, quite unconsciously, a change in their routine. Their normal practice was for them to circulate in separate spheres but today they felt they couldn't bear to be apart, and they toured their guests together in an aura of happiness that clung to them like a musky scent.

They were now approaching their old and close friends Lord and Lady Mallaby. Angela Mallaby was so relieved at the news of Betty's marriage that she was, for once, over-loud in her congratulations at the news; so, in order to get off the subject, Diana asked her if she had heard yet about becoming a local magistrate.

'I've heard on the grapevine,' Angela answered, 'that the county committee have put my name forward. I'm told that that's progress, but I've heard nothing officially.'

'In that case,' said Diana, 'you'd better come along with me.'

Diana had spotted the judge, standing on his own and looking up at the portrait of Effie Grey, and it was to him that she now introduced Angela.

'Lady Mallaby is hoping to join the Somersham bench,' she told him.

'Indeed?' He twinkled at Diana. 'I might have known, dear Duchess, that I could rely on you not to forget my little suggestion.'

Diana left them deep in talk about the judiciary, conscious that another small piece of business was satisfactorily on its way. Meanwhile, Rupert and Andrew Mallaby had been left on their own, standing companionably in silence. Then Andrew laughed.

'Look over there,' he said, pointing across the room.

Rupert's eyes followed his finger. Dame Elizabeth

de Blete, clad in a voluminous dress of drab olive with a clanking spiked necklace contrived out of wrought iron, was moving up to Lorna Jordans, icily elegant in a gun-metal sheath of jersey wool.

'My mother and Dame E.?' said Rupert. 'What about them?'

'They look like an old dreadnought coming into berth next to a fast modern cruiser.' Lord Mallaby had served his time in the Royal Navy. 'And between them they command more fire-power than anyone else in the county.'

'You're so right,' Rupert agreed, 'but to see them now, you'd never think so.'

Both men began to move in the direction of the two ladies. As they jostled through the crowd, the thought came to Rupert that it was very odd about Dame Elizabeth. The old girl must have known about his affair; he knew from experience that her intelligence service missed nothing of consequence in Mallamshire. She was a true friend, and she spoke her mind: why, then, had she refrained from tackling him? From all appearances, the Dame had stood aside, letting events take their course, which was most unlike her. But then, he added to himself, she was getting on a bit in years: it was only natural that perhaps her consuming interest in reducing to order what she called untidiness in human affairs was on the wane.

Dame Elizabeth, meanwhile, was addressing her friend and ally, Lorna.

'I must say,' she boomed, 'it is a very satisfactory conclusion to an unfortunate episode. I congratulate you.'

'Me? I don't know what I've done. After all, it was you who persuaded me to change my mind and invite Betty to the Dower House; and it was your idea to make sure Colin was there.'

'It was an outside chance,' said the Dame, 'but it

worked. I've seen something of the kind before, you know: a girl thinks she's in love with one brother when in fact she's much more taken with the other. Sometimes, and tragically, she doesn't realise in time; it was fortunate that your luncheon jolted Betty into a realisation of the mistake she was making.'

'Betty is a delightful woman, and she will make Colin an excellent wife. All in all, I'm happy for them both.'

'Of course you are. After all,' the Dame teased, 'it would have been a dreadful shame to pass up the chance of scooping all Betty's dollars into the family coffers.'

'You may laugh, Dame E., but I don't regard money as a laughing matter. Colin is a younger son; and I could never have provided for him as amply as will his wife.'

'Anyway,' said the Dame changing the subject, 'both Rupert and Diana have come through it all – and Diana with flying colours. My admiration for Diana grows every day: and in my view, she handled a horrid situation with skill and courage.'

'I agree. And I take it that maybe your esteem for Rupert is a bit diminished.'

'Not, really, Lorna. He was thoughtless and self-indulgent; but he came to his senses in time, and you have only to look at them both now to see how good their marriage is.'

'You're more tolerant than I am, Dame E. When I feared that Rupert might have been following in his father's footsteps, I could cheerfully have throttled him! I know I'm his mother and ought to take his side right or wrong, but he was wrong and I told him so.'

They had now to break off, for Rupert himself was approaching. As he did so, the photographer from the *Gazette*, who had been weaving in and out of the assembly, flashed his camera at the group. This gave Rupert an idea.

'Why don't we have a group photograph taken?' he

suggested. 'We ought to record old Colin's marriage for posterity. And we'll have it taken like one of the old pictures, with the whole family posed formally on the steps of the portico.'

'That's a lovely idea,' said Diana, who had come up to join arms with Rupert, 'and we must have the staff too – just like the old days.'

Dobson looked a bit stunned when instructed to leave the party as he was to have his photograph taken: but, still clutching his salver, he progressed out to the portico, while James the footman was despatched to the bowels of the house to fetch out old Aggie Smiles. Rupert, meanwhile, was going round the rooms cutting out those he wanted to join in the posed picture, like a sheepdog working his flock.

Colin and Tom de Blete brought out some chairs, which they arranged in a row under the centre of the pediment. Here, with the sun at its high June zenith, deep shadows cast into sharp relief the soaring stone columns, and in this shade the assembly milled about, until Rupert called them to order and began to give instructions as to where each should take a place.

It is a fine group photograph that appeared on the back page of the *Mallamshire Gazette*. In the foreground, on the stone steps with their legs crossed and dressed in identical shirts and shorts, sit the eight-year-old Charles, by courtesy Earl of Rockport, and his brother Lord Jonathan. Standing at the back, on one side are ranged Dobson, his eyebrows beetling at the camera, the hump-backed James, and, a dumpy figure half hidden in the shadows, Mrs Smiles, who has forgotten to remove her apron. On the other side, representing the administration, Tom de Blete is flanked by Jean and Mark Wright (the latter appearing in his role as Duke's cousin): in the middle, peering over her mistress's shoulders, is placed Molly Platt, with the nurserymaid skulking in her shade.

On the row of chairs, Rupert Duke of Jordans takes pride of place in the very centre. He has Diana his duchess on his right hand and Lorna his mother on his left, with Lord Colin at one end and Lady Colin at the other.

Dame Elizabeth de Blete, who was watching from the gravelled forecourt, felt a deep sense of satisfaction. The family group, as formal, symmetrical and deliberately composed as the facade of the great house that rose above them. Yet, just as the magnificent building needed constant attention and ever-running repairs, so also did the relationships represented in the photograph. Nothing showed now of the cracks that had once threatened to bring the whole edifice crashing to the ground; for the group now staring into the camera's lens represented stability, continuity, the handing down from generation to generation of tradition and of obligation. The Dame was pleased; for she knew now that the House of Jordans was in good hands.